DOUG PARKER

RITES
→ OF →
PASSAGE

Many special thanks to E.J. Hammon, A.F. Presson, and D. Lopez for all their wonderful insights and support.

First Edition Published February 2021
ISBN: 978-0-992266-20-2

Cover designed by MiblArt.

Contents

Chapter 1

"WHERE ARE WE GOING AGAIN?" I asked the smiling blonde goddess who pulled me by the hand through the woods.

"To the party, silly," said Bethany.

I pointed towards the faint music, laughter and wood smoke. "Isn't the swim team kegger that way?"

"Yes," she said. "But that's for later. I'm talking about our party."

A flash of white showed itself between the trees, and I pulled her to a stop. "Wait. There's someone's house up ahead."

She pulled her hand out of mine. "Come on, Cas. Do you think I'm an in-the-dirt kinda girl?" She laughed and ran towards the house.

I jogged after her and broke through the treeline. Someone had built a two-story McMansion in the woods outside of Greensboro, and someone else had tried to burn it down. Weathered smoke stains trailed upwards from broken windows covered with rotting plywood. The front porch boasted a pair of solid wood double doors eight feet high, and a pile of debris to match. Full-grown hickory trees pierced a once-manicured lawn, and the setting summer sun hovered in the tree-tops, casting a pall of shadows that sent a shiver up my spine.

Bethany waved to me from the doors. "Come on, slow-poke. Give me a hand, they're stuck."

She stepped aside as I reached the porch. I twisted the door handle and heaved. The door's hinges squealed in protest as it grated open. "There," I said. "Now we—"

Magic flared behind me. A force grabbed me and shoved me through the doorway. The door slammed shut. Picking myself up from the floor, I heard Bethany and someone else laughing and cheering. A small avalanche hit the door as they pushed over the debris pile outside.

I punched the smoke-scarred front door. Calling out that it wasn't funny locking a guy in a crumbling ruin was pointless. Bethany and whoever were leaving, laughing at the new guy, locked away when he thought he might have made friends this time. The memory of being trapped in my gym locker for hours swamped my mind.

I took a deep breath and popped a globe to brighten up the place. The globe was fuzzy and an ugly shade of orange, but at least I could see. The entry hall and its grand staircase were covered in burnt everything. Darkness lurked in the other rooms, except one. Elanor stepped into the entry hall, her own globe of light casting her trim figure in clear silver.

"Did you put him up to this?" she demanded.

I shook my head. "You're not the only one who got played. Him who?"

"Jacob."

"Really?"

"We used to be friends. I thought… well, I was an idiot. I warned you about Bethany."

I turned back to the double doors, blackened and unyielding. "Yeah, but you're my magic tutor, not my love doctor."

"Screw you."

My knuckles throbbed. I'd hoped Bethany was different. The phone calls and hallway flirts. An almost kiss after gym before her friends snatched her away. Then the Sending, full of warm emotion and promised soft skin. I punched the door again, harder.

"Does that help?" Elanor asked, tying her cloud of red hair into a ponytail.

"No."

"Well, I'm sure they've blocked the door somehow. Come on. We need to find another way out before that door breaks your hand."

"I don't know. Those jerks might wait for us to crawl out through a mud pit to get yearbook photos."

"Sounds like you've had that experience already."

I looked back to see her brown eyes looking askance at my crappy orange globe. "When it comes to assholes, I'm the expert."

She sighed. "You want me to Send to my parents for help?"

"No." I stepped away from the door. "I mean to leave the same way I came in." I let my globe go and dove deeper into the magic than I did at school, creating an enormous fist in my mind.

Elanor frowned. "What are you—?"

The magic coursed through me; the fist fuzzed, then cleared and formed diamond hard. I slammed it into the door. A cloud of ash exploded over me, burning my eyes. Coughing, I spat soot from my mouth.

Elanor waved away the ash cloud. "You idiot! Are you trying to knock this place down on us? What the hell?"

"This place is fine. Another good hit and we're free."

"So big yellow signs saying keep out, building condemned, mean something different where you come from?"

Part of the ceiling plaster crashed onto the staircase.

"Look. I'm sorry, okay? Now if you don't want to get your dress dirty, back up."

"Wait." She held up her hand and pointed behind me. "What is that?"

The cracks in the doors gave a green glow that pulsed like a slow heartbeat. My hands clenched into fists. "Those bastards! I thought they left!"

Elanor shook her head. "I don't think they're doing that. That doesn't look…."

I took a breath and tried to use my magic to see what she was seeing. Nothing but fuzz. I shook my head. "So what is it then? I can't see any details."

"Well, obviously it's a ward. More than that, I can't say; you swamped this area with your backwash."

"Okay, so let's try another room. If it is them, they can't cover the entire house, it's too big."

Elanor turned and stormed off. Following behind, I saw empty shelves lining the walls. A library, once upon a time. She pivoted, her globe reddening.

"No. I'm going this way. I'm going to take my time and be careful. You go that way. If you won't sit on your hands and wait, at least you won't collapse the house on me. I already feel like a fool, I don't need to be a dead fool on top of it."

"Look, I'm sorry alright? If you want to Send for help, go ahead. It'll take your folks time to get here, so—"

"I already tried! The ward is blocking me, everything!" Elanor strode out of the library, leaving the darkness to swallow me.

"Come on!" I called to her. "We're locked in a run-down mansion with no way of getting help, and the first thing you do is split the party?"

Her voice echoed down the hall. "Leave me alone, orphan!"

I popped a globe, fuzzy and tinged with green, and stomped the other way. My nails pressed deep into my palms. Getting played by the popular kids sucked, but it wasn't exactly new to either of us. Being better at magic than the teachers hung a target on her back as much as constantly being the 'new kid' hung one on mine.

I found the remains of the kitchen. Double doors, devoid of glass but boarded up, led outside. Walking towards them, the floor groaned and dipped under my feet. I jumped backwards as the blackened bulk of the fridge toppled forward and crunched into the floor.

"Okay. So this place is a deathtrap. Great."

I focused on the doors, but my globe's green glow wasn't helping. Plunging myself back into darkness, I gave my real eyes a minute to adjust before trying my magic ones. Clean and clear, yes!

The doors had a solid green glow. I could faintly see a few green threads, like holding thin fabric up to a bright light, but nothing I could work with.

"Hope you're having better luck, Elanor."

She must be terrified. The dark corridor back beckoned. No. Best to leave her alone right now. Shaking my head to clear my eyes, I popped another globe.

The kitchen floor cracked open, and the fridge slid down, crashing into the darkness below. Easing the globe over the hole, I saw the fridge on its side, laying on a tiled floor.

"Basement. And basements sometimes have doors."

The kitchen had another door, this one inside the house. The laundry? The floor firmed up as I got closer. The hinges squeaked, and I had to pull hard to open it. Uncharred steps descended into the darkness.

I stomped hard on the first step, getting a muffled but firm thump. Walking down, the basement wasn't burnt, but soot dusted everything. It was also brighter than my globe alone should have made it.

"Well, alright." Trails in the floor dust led me to an exterior door hanging half off its hinges, letting in the last of the sunlight. I tried my magic eyes. Fuzzy, but clear enough to show the ward covering the door.

9

"Too weird. No way the entire swim team is out there doing this."

I wanted to check-in with Elanor. Hopefully she'd calmed down enough that I could talk to her. Wait. That string in the ward. It looked important. I glanced at the kitchen fridge that now lived in the basement.

"Okay. Not so much oomph this time."

I tried to pop a knife aligned with the ward's magic. It formed, but kept threatening to fuzz out. Hoping it was sharp enough, I reached forward and tested it against the thread.

A shriek, filled with all the petulant rage of a tortured child, blasted me off my feet. I tried to roll and stand, but the ground was the ceiling. No globe, no knife, just darkness and fear. Chest heaving, sucking in air, I tried to find the floor. Darkness outlined in fire rose in the shape of a giant. An arm lashed out and smashed into me. Something inside my chest burned. I popped a globe, bright as the sun. The creature shrieked, but backed up. It looked away, then hissed at me and flew through the ceiling.

Elanor!

Chapter 2

CHARGING UP THE STAIRS, I couldn't Send her a warning. "Dammit! Elanor!" My throat was raw. My feet punched holes in the kitchen floor as I sprinted back to the main hall. "Elanor!"

"Cas!"

The giant filled the corridor. Elanor was backing up as the creature stomped forward, tearing through some barrier that shattered like glass but kept reforming.

"Get out of there!" I smashed the giant with my globe. It screamed and my globe burst. Pain ripped through my skull from the feedback.

"Cas! Cast another globe! Big as you can!"

I tried to pop another, but it spluttered and died.

"Cas!"

I screamed and dove deep. The globe cleared and light flared, bringing the hallway into sharp relief. A web of magic from Elanor snared my globe. My magic poured through without end, like I was vomiting and couldn't stop. Elanor's crystal barrier snapped into focus, glass threads strong as diamond. The creature railed against the barrier but it held firm, a giant crystal statue filled with darkness, fire, and rage.

The torrent eased. Gasping, I found myself on the floor, my heart pounding in my ears. Elanor was next to me. "Cas! Are you okay?"

"Yeah." I tried to swallow. "I'm okay." With help, I rolled onto my back. "Everything hurts, but I'm okay. Are you okay?"

"Yes, I'm fine." She slumped against the wall and hugged her knees.

I could sense the giant's rage scratch at the barrier like an ice pick down my spine. Sitting up, I leaned against the wall next to Elanor and waited for the world to stop spinning.

"What the hell is that?" I asked.

"It must be a ghost. Did you find a body somewhere?"

"It attacked me in the basement, and no, I didn't see a body. There was a door, though, to outside. Looks like someone else forced it open."

"Was it warded?"

"Yeah," I said.

"But you tried to punch it."

"No." I hung my head. "I could see a thread pretty clearly, so I tried to cut it. Then sparkles here jumped me."

Elanor shook her head. "I told you not to mess around."

"At least I didn't bring the house down on you."

"This time."

I smiled. She chuckled. We both laughed. "Aw man," I said, wiping tears from my eyes. "I'm sorry."

She smiled. "Thank you."

"Any time." The ghost stared at us with eyes like hot coals. "So, it looks like this place is haunted for real."

Elanor tucked a strand of her long red hair back behind her ear. "I don't know why. I didn't sense any recent death or trauma when I was checking things."

"How did you do that?" I pointed at the ghost frozen in glass. "How did you even do that? There's nothing like that in any textbook I've ever seen."

Brown eyes stared at mine for a moment. She shrugged. "It's not a huge secret. Okay, basic biomancy. You're born with no magic, get a small touch when you're nine, then a big bump when you hit puberty, right?"

"Yeah."

"Well, I skipped that last part."

My eyes wanted to wander down, but I forced them to stay locked on hers. "Not to be creepy, but I've never thought you missed puberty." She looked away, a hint of red on her cheeks. Oh crap. Where the hell did that come from? "Okay," I said. "That was super creepy. I'm sorry."

"Yes, it was." She sighed. "What I meant was that my magic never got a bump, not a big one anyway. In terms of raw power, I'm not much stronger than a twelve-year-old. My parents took me out of school and sent me to tons of specialists, to help me draw more, but I couldn't. They even got a Fae."

"A Fae? Wow! How the hell did they manage that?"

Elanor shrugged. "My dad works for the government. He's a part of the consulate program, so he has connections. This Fae was a pretty nice guy, actually. He did something like what I did to your globe. First he apologized, then pulled power from me until I blacked out."

"I felt like my insides were coming out."

"Me too. It didn't help. He declared my conduit blocked and there was nothing to be done. I spent the next three years with specialists, learning to cast as efficiently as possible. By the time I came back, it was sophomore year in high school and everyone was different."

"Like Jacob."

She nodded. "Yes. We were close before. We even went on a date once, but then...." She stood up and pulled me to my feet. "When you showed up, the school made me give up my study-hall time to help you. I wondered if he was jealous because that's when he started talking like the Jacob I knew before."

13

Magic thrummed through me as she tweaked something on the creature's crystalline cage. "But that was all B.S., obviously. Just like these wards and this ghost."

"How so?" I asked.

"These wards are self-maintaining, which is impossible; and the longest record of a ghost surviving postmortem is three days. But there's no trace of any violent death since the fire ten years ago."

"Could the ward be here to trap the ghost?"

"Possibly, but kids have snuck in here for years and nothing has ever happened." She shrugged. "Then again, you tried to wreck the place; maybe it was some long dormant defense?"

"Oh, man," I said. "What if, when the fire happened, the wards popped up and everyone inside couldn't get out?"

Elanor shook her head. "No. You can set a ward to let certain auras through. It's not that hard. Apart from being self-sustaining, the rest of the ward structure looks fairly conventional. If it was a defense for the family that lived here, they should have been able to get through."

I nodded. "So I've unleashed a horror from beyond the grave. What did you do today?"

Elanor's laugh was contagious. "Well," she said after a minute. "I may have found us a way out of this horror movie. I found a book with a faint aura that matches the ward, before that thing attacked me."

I followed her into a room with the charred remains of a child's bed. She picked up a book, blackened by the fire. "Damn, it's washed out. I was hoping we could use it as a key."

I tried to look with my magic eyes. My head throbbed, and I grabbed the wall to keep from falling over. "Sorry. I can't cast anything right now."

"I'm surprised you're standing. That's a heavy draw you're maintaining." She looked down. "I'm sorry about forcing you like that, but it was the only way."

"We're both alive, so it's all good. Just shout 'battery' the next time you need to use me as one, okay?"

"It's a deal," she said.

"Good. Come on, then. If there was one key, maybe there's another. But this time we'll look together."

She nodded. "The ground floor of this wing is useless from all the power we used to trap the ghost bleeding everywhere. Probably the upstairs, too."

"I pulled a lot of magic when it attacked me in the basement. What about the second floor at that end? Surely that should be enough distance to keep things intact."

She shrugged. "It's our best shot, let's go."

We paused in the entry hall at the foot of the once-grand staircase. Blackness enveloped us as Elanor doused her globe.

"You want us to search in the dark?"

"That book had an imprint, but it was very faint. We can't risk any magic right now in case it washes out the one thing that's our ticket out of this place."

The burnt steps crunched as we made our way up to the second floor, the railing charred under my palm. My stomach lurched as power pulled through me and I had to stop, chest heaving.

"I feel it too," said Elanor, her hand gripping my shoulder. "The ghost is trying to force the cage. Are you okay?"

I nodded. "Yeah, just watch out in case last week's breakfast makes an appearance."

We made it to the landing and headed away from the ghost. The corridor was pure darkness. I shuffled forward, hand on the wall, feeling my way until the ash-smooth wall gave way to charred wood.

"Door," I said.

"Okay. You stay here, I'll go in and check."

As Elanor opened the door, moonlight flooded the hall. The plywood covering the windows must have fallen away, and the interior was full of dark debris. She walked to the center of the room and slowly turned, searching.

The power tugged again, trying to drag me deeper. My chest burned like I was drowning. My chest? Oh my god, my chest! I pulled off my shirt. The moonlight tinted everything, but there was nothing where the ghost hit me. No bruising, no tenderness, no mark.

"I don't know what the hell you think you're doing, but this is seriously not the time or place."

I looked up to see Elanor staring at me, anger and disgust on her face, clutching a child's doll.

"No. No, this isn't—"

"I've had enough of you and your lies, why the hell are you so horrible?" She rushed past me. "What did I do to you?"

"Elanor! Wait!" I stumbled through the corridor after her. Crunching down the steps, I tumbled onto the entry hall floor as the spiteful giant shrieked and pulled so hard I almost blacked out. Elanor stood by the main door, staring at the doll. She screamed, then collapsed and sobbed.

I sat up and sucked down air enough to breathe.

"Everything is shit," I said. "But I'm not lying to you about anything. What is going on?"

"I find out I'm a freak, because my conduit is smaller than a twelve-year-old's. I finally come back to school to find that everyone has changed and everyone hates me. I'm so good at using what magic I have that I get to skip magic class to work on college courses, which makes everyone think I'm a nerd and hate me even more. I could have graduated after summer school and said goodbye to this train wreck. But then you show up, completely useless, and I'm forced to spend my college prep time on you." She points towards the cracked front doors.

"Yet since we've been here, you've cast some major spells and are sustaining a ward that three people would struggle with. I don't know what the hell is going on, but I want out." She held up the doll. "I even have the key. But it's too weak for both of us to use. So only one of us gets to leave, and if I go then you die."

My chest was so tight I almost couldn't speak. Breathe in. Breathe out. In. "Yes, I pulled a lot of power. And I need your help because it's only when I dive that deep that anything works right." In. Out. In. "I can't do the low-power stuff they teach at school. It fuzzes out unless I pump it up, but then the construct breaks." In. Out. In. "You're the first person who seems to give a damn about helping me get a handle on things since I was nine. I'm not lying to you about anything." My chest loosened as the ghost settled in its cage.

Elanor stared at the doll, then looked up at me. "So what's with the Captain Naked routine?"

"When the ghost attacked me in the basement, it hit me. It felt like I was on fire, but it went away. I wanted to see how bad it was." I shook my head. "It doesn't look like anything though."

Elanor put the doll down, then came over and knelt by me. A globe little bigger than a candle flame appeared, revealing her face scrunched in curiosity. I looked down at my chest. I'm no muscle-bound meathead, but all the hours of swim practice had me looking decent. She reached out and the touch of her warm fingertips sent a shock up my spine and raised the hairs on the back of my neck. I focused on the doll, its messy dark hair adrift on the floor and the painted smile trying to convince me it was my friend. Breathe in, breathe out. In. Out.

"No physical trauma I can sense," she said.

"Well, it hurt like hell." I swallowed. "It's kinda creepy how you know so much about ghosts, corpses, and how to magically look for physical trauma."

"I'm working on getting into a magical forensics program," she said. Her eyes narrowed and she pressed her fingertips against my sternum. "Does that hurt?"

"No more than it should. Can I put my shirt on now?"

Elanor froze. She whipped her hand away and doused her globe. I put my shirt on.

"You take the doll and go," she said. "I can at least keep it at bay."

"No way. I saw it busting through your shield. Even if I could Send to my foster parents, by the time they get here you'd be dead."

"Well, if I leave, the ghost's ward breaks and that thing will be all over you."

"I fought it off in the basement."

"It had another target to attack. Besides, that was before. You're exhausted now, I can see it. Can you honestly keep up a full assault for the half-hour it'll take for help to get here, plus however long it takes for someone to unravel the ward from the outside?"

She was right. "Well, I'm not leaving." I felt the ghost coiling in its prison. "So if you're not leaving either, we need to find another solution because—" I winced as it tried to drag me under. "Because I'm not sure how much longer I can keep this up."

Chapter 3

ELANOR PUT HER HAND ON HER CHIN, biting her lip like when she was solving a math problem. "You got hit, but there's no trauma. When it left you to attack me, did it go up the stairs?"

"No," I said. "It flew through the ceiling."

She snapped her fingers. "No wonder it's weird. It's incorporeal, a being of pure aura." She began pacing. "That's why your light globe hurt it, because the power you were pumping through it threatens its core stability!"

Elanor stalked back to the imprisoned giant. I stumbled along, trying to keep up. Leaning against the wall, I felt her reach out to the giant's prison. Pins and needles danced up my arms as she tweaked and tucked, then something tore and my load shifted, lightened. My chest loosened, and I breathed freely.

"That feels better, thanks," I said. The ghost raged against its cage, but the prison held and the ice picks felt more distant. "What did you do?"

"I stripped out the physical component of the ward." Bright brown eyes looked at me. "I was sure it would work!"

I popped my magic goggles, clean and clear and rather easy for a change. The spider's web encasing the ghost was visible, but gave no clue to how I could spin one. The ghost itself was still darkness and fire, but I could see it pulse like a heartbeat, like... "You know, the ghost's aura looks identical to the ward's."

"Yes. They're definitely linked."

"Which means the doll's also linked, right? That's why we can use it as a key. But auras fade after a few hours, it couldn't have an imprint after ten years."

"Not unless something kept refreshing it." Elanor frowned. "Which could only be the ghost. Which means the ghost could leave anytime it wanted to." She shook her head. "Though it would probably fade as soon as it got outside."

"Do you remember anything about the fire here? Was it an accident or..."

"No idea. I was around six years old. Why?"

"Because whoever set the ward to sustain the ghost may have murdered an entire family to do it."

Elanor shook her head. "I don't know. Using death energies to power a ward as a battery of sorts? I've never heard of anything like that."

"Something to think about while we wait for help, I guess." I sat down against the wall. "Someone will come looking, eventually."

We sat in silence. The events of the last half-hour tumbled in my mind.

"I wish I had a cell phone," said Elanor. "I doubt the ward would block it."

"Hah! Me too. Though with our luck it wouldn't get a signal out here in the woods."

"My dad has one," said Elanor. "He says it's pretty good in most places. Considering how much trouble you have using magic to send messages, I'm surprised the state didn't give you one."

I snorted. "Your dad works for the government and can get a Fae tutor to help his daughter. I'm an orphan who needs to stop being lazy and learn how to cast like everyone else."

Elanor's lips pursed. "Fae."

"What?"

"Something I remember from my tutors. Fae can link their magic to things or events."

"You're saying this whole thing is Fae work?"

"I don't know." She paced. "What I do know is that because the doll, the ghost, and the ward are linked, it's possible to amalgamate the ghost and the doll. That'll boost the doll's aura so we can both escape!"

"Amalgamate."

"Yes, mesh them together!"

"You're going to possess the doll with the ghost."

"Yes."

"And why is this a better choice than waiting for help?"

Elanor walked over and pulled me up. "Because if this is Fae work, it might take days to unravel. If either of us passes out, we're dead." Brown eyes met mine. "And from the look of you, we've only got a few hours before you fall over."

While the drain was lighter, I couldn't deny the mounting exhaustion. "So, how do we get the ghost to possess the doll?"

"Well," she said as we returned to the foyer. "I'll take the doll to the other end of the house. It's going to take me a minute to set up the ghost trap, and I can't do that while I'm maintaining the ward."

"So I'm blocking the ghost while you fall back for a Hail Mary play."

"Yes, and you need to delay as long as you can because if I move too fast the doll's baseline aura will wash out and we won't have a key."

"I hate ball-sports." I frowned. "I also can't get too close to you, or whatever I'm doing might destroy the key."

Elanor nodded and picked up the doll. "It's our only shot."

We passed the kitchen. Next up was a lounge full of boarded-up windows and an unburnt patch of carpet. Two doors lead into other rooms. "Looks like an office, and a bedroom," I said. "What's your pick?"

"Bedroom," said Elanor. "A little more room to work in there. Oh hey, an ensuite between the two of them."

Sure enough, a bathroom as big as my bedroom joined the two. I shook my head. "I could do laps in that tub."

Elanor was studying the lounge. "Try not to come closer than where the sofa used to be," she said, pointing to the mark in the carpet.

"Okay."

"So I guess, good luck?"

I nodded. "I'll need a minute before you start."

She held out her hand. I took it and squeezed gently, her soft skin chilled by the dampness. I tried to smile, to ease the worry lines around those beautiful brown eyes. She smiled back, squeezed my hand, then took the doll into the bedroom.

Walking towards the ghost, my chest was tight and my fingertips dug into my palms. Breathe in, breathe out. Treat this like a meet and my heat is up next. I can't spin a web like Elanor did, and it can dodge my globes. "Okay sparkles. You in your lane," I said, rubbing my hands together. "And me in mine."

Elanor's shout from the other end of the house was muffled. Her touch on the ghost's prison was not. It bulged as she cut off my power flow. The ghost shrieked, and the prison exploded in crystalline shards. Darkness and fire loomed over me.

"Not today," I said. I formed a long rope, a living lane guide, and dove for the power to embody it. It formed bright and clear. The ghost flew at me and I cracked the rope like a whip, forcing it off. It turned to go after Elanor, but I looped the rope around it and guided it back to me. Its shriek hammered my head and spots danced before my eyes. It swooped, and I dove to the floor, keeping the rope between us, the loop closing in on the ghost from behind. The ghost tore past me, the rope bright and shining between us.

I rolled to my feet as the ghost ducked out of the loop. It lashed out with an arm of fire that caught me on my back. An ice pick in my spine, molten pain burning me whole. My rope spluttered as the pain mounted. I shortened it to a whip and attacked. It wrapped around the ghost's neck. I pulled, and it dove forward, a blackened fist crashing into my face.

I'm on the floor, chest heaving. Pain clawing through my every nerve. The ghost. Where is it? I clamber to my feet and try to run. I can't scream. Kitchen. Lounge. Bedroom. Elanor stands in the doorway to the bathroom, rigid. The ghost, screaming, has its arms wrapped around her. A tendril of blue fire connects the ghost to the doll in the corner. I pop a knife and jump. The knife slices through the ghost's arms as I tackle Elanor, and we go crashing into the ensuite. The ghost's scream pierces my eardrums as a flare of blue light illuminates the room, then there is nothing but the sound of our breathing.

I rolled over and sat up. Elanor's eyes are wide, still struggling with the ghost, her teeth bared in a tight-lipped smile. Then her body went limp like a cut string.

I shook her. "Elanor!"

She opened her eyes and smiled. "It worked."

"Never had a doubt," I said.

"It's fully enmeshed with the doll."

"Strong enough to get us both out?"

"And then some, yes."

I helped her up. "Then let's get—" Something shattered. There, in the doorway to the bedroom, stood the doll. It's happy, friendly painted-on face cocked sideways, a long shard of broken glass clutched in one hand.

Chapter 4

ELANOR SCREAMED. Grabbing her hand, I pulled her through into the office. I slammed the door closed, kicking up a cloud of ash which burnt my eyes. We stumbled into the lounge; the doll waiting in front of us. Its shriek drove us back. I tripped over something and we fell down in a heap, coughing dust.

The ash cloud settled. The doll stood at the doorway to the office. The disembodied scream rattled my head and darkness consumed me.

My head throbbed and my throat was raw. Elanor was on the floor next to me, mouth open, eyes fixated. I sat up and saw the doll still standing at the doorway between the office and the lounge, glass shard in hand.

"Are you okay?" I said, reaching out to Elanor. She flinched when I touched her arm, still staring at the doll. "Elanor. Please, say something."

She twitched, then looked at me. "You're alive," she whispered. She clung to me, and I to her. "Oh my god. I thought you were dead! You weren't moving or breathing or—"

"I'm okay, I'm okay." I took her face in my hands. "I'm alive and I'm okay, and so are you."

It took a moment, but she nodded. "Yes. Yes, I am." Worried brown eyes met mine. I could almost see the spark within her flare back to life. "Why are we still alive?"

"I don't know." The office had a boarded-up window. I flipped on my magic goggles, fuzzy but good enough to see that the ward still blocked the window. The doorway to the lounge was unblocked. "It should've come in by now. There's nothing to stop it."

Elanor frowned. "It doesn't want to come in." She stood up. "Maybe there's something in here that can tell us why." There wasn't much to go through. The metal frame of the desk still stood but little else, so we shoved the ash piles around. "Here," said Elanor.

It was a picture frame; the glass smoked-stained and broken, but the picture was intact. Taking the picture out revealed a beautiful family smiling at us from the fire-singed photo. Husband, wife, and two young girls who must have been twins.

"I think you're right, Cas. The ghost is one of the family members, one of the daughters."

"Yeah? How so?"

"My father is a great guy, but his work is very hush-hush. When I was younger, my parents were very strict about not going into his office without permission. Even now if the door's closed I have to knock and wait." She sighed. "It's closed a lot lately."

The photo held no other clues. "We can't get past the ward," I said. "And a possessed doll is waiting to murder us if we leave this room. Do you have any ideas about how to get out of here?"

Elanor shook her head. "I never expected it to enmesh so strongly it would animate. It must have a huge energy reserve to do that." She sighed. "We need to touch the doll to use it as a key, but physically it's fragile. If we grab and wrestle it we might break it, which would release the ghost and lose us any hope of getting out of here."

"And get stabbed for our troubles."

"Yes," she said. "That too."

"Could you use telekinesis? You can use me as a battery if you need."

"No." She slouched on the remains of the desk. "I mean I could, but the same problem exists. It would resist, using its considerable magical strength, and chances are we would destroy the doll in the struggle." She shrugged. "So I got nothing."

I turned towards the doll. "I don't remember if my family was this nice," I said as I sat down in front of it. I put the photo on the floor. "I was six when they died in a car crash, probably about how old you were when they took this photo."

"Cas," said Elanor. "What are you doing?"

"Talking." I looked at the doll's painted-on smile. "Got nothing else to do so we might as well, right?" The doll cocked its head at me.

"My name is Cassius," I said. "You can call me Cas if you want to. This is Elanor, my friend." I pointed to one girl in the photo. "Was this you?"

The doll's head tilted down, then shook.

"No? So this one then?"

The head nodded.

Elanor sat beside me. "Oh my god," she whispered. "It's communicating."

"She," I said. "She is talking with me," I smiled at the doll. "Right?"

More nodding, a little more enthusiastically.

"I'm very sorry for coming into your home without asking," I said. "And for trying to break stuff." The doll raised the hand full of jagged glass. "I was scared, and I was trying to get out. You know what that feels like, don't you?" The hand lowered. A single nod.

"Elanor and I, we were tricked by some other kids who are not very nice." A wave of anger surged from the doll and washed over me. "Did someone not very nice do this to you?"

The doll spun and raged, shattering the glass shard against the door frame, then it turned and ran.

"Please don't go," called Elanor. The doll stopped in the middle of the lounge, then plopped down, hands holding its head, shaking.

"Please stay," I said. "I know what it's like to be alone." The doll looked at me. "My parents died when I was your age, so I had to live with other families as I grew up. They seemed okay, but they always fell apart, and I always had to go on to another family." My throat tightened. "I never had anyone for very long. I figured that was it for me."

Elanor squeezed my shoulder. "Really?"

I nodded. "My first foster family had me until I was almost nine. Then having a second kid to look after was too much. They got a divorce, and I got moved on. After that, every six months, whatever family I get placed with breaks up. They all look nice, but underneath everything is rotten." I snorted. "Like Bethany. Pretty on the surface but rotten in her core."

The doll came back and sat in front of me. I risked a moment to try on my magic goggles. The doll's soul was still dark, but the fire seemed to have gone.

"And Jacob," said Elanor. "The boy who tricked me."

"Yes, he's not very nice." I leaned closer to the doll. "His breath smells funny," I whispered. "I think he likes to eat rotten pickles!"

The doll shook and I could almost feel a giggle. Elanor raised her eyebrow at me.

"I lived in a group home for a while, with other orphans. Sometimes, the young ones cried in the night and it helped to talk to them." I swallowed. "Sometimes the one crying was me." Elanor held my hand, and then plastic fingers touched my knee. The doll had crossed the threshold into the office.

"Elanor thinks she knows how to get out of here, but we need your help," I said. "Will you help us?" The doll nodded.

"I'm sorry," said Elanor. "For scaring you when I trapped you in the doll. I hope I didn't hurt you."

We stood up, and the doll raised its arms. My heart pounded like a sledgehammer when I picked it up, but it settled against me. We walked to the kitchen, then down into the basement. Moonlight shone through the open basement door to the outside world.

Elanor took the doll's hand in her own. "I don't know what's going to happen when we walk through," she said. "Cas and I should be able to leave, but I don't know what will happen to you."

The doll trembled in my arms, but nodded and pointed to the doorway.

"Okay," I said. We walked through, together.

Cool night air greeted us. A night bird called and cicadas hummed. I let out a deep breath I didn't realize I was holding. The doll was limp and lifeless. Elanor looked back. "Cas," she said.

I turned. A young girl, a little older than the photo, stood outside the doorway. She was already fading away. "Thank you," she said. "Please. Find my sister."

I nodded. "Of course I will. What happened to her?"

"The bad man took her," she said. "Before."

"Before what?" said Elanor.

"The fire," whispered the ghost. She faded, fuzzed, and disappeared.

Leaves rustled in a breeze as the moon hid behind a passing cloud. The insects trilled and Elanor turned to me.

"The ward's gone," she said. "Like it was never even there. Not a trace of an aura or anything."

We followed the crumbling driveway back to the main road.

"There's a convenience store about a half-mile that way," I said. "That's where the bus dropped me off."

Elanor nodded. "I'll Send to my parents when we get there," she said. "Right now, I want to walk and breathe."

"So," I said. "Should we try somewhere a little less dangerous for our second date?"

She laughed. Then she put her hand in mine. "Sounds like a plan," she said, smiling.

Chapter 5

SITTING ON THE BED I STARED at Elanor's letters on the cork board above the desk. It had been three weeks since the end of school and Elanor went on a two-week road trip with her parents. The first letter arrived the day after she left. She talked about how excited she was to spend time with her parents, especially her dad. She worried about how boring it was going to be. She complained that her hand hurt from so much writing since I wasn't able to chat by magic. It smelled faintly of her perfume and the dots on the I's were little hearts.

The second letter came a week later. The first stops were more fun than she expected. Her parents were great. No scent. No hearts. She said she missed me.

The third letter was a postcard from some national park. Everything was fine. Hope you're having a great summer. The end.

Nobody answered the phone at her house. No calls for me here. Back a week and nothing. Hearts and perfume to nothing in three weeks. Story of My Life.

David knocked on the open door. "Hey Cas. It looks like it might rain. Did you need a ride?"

"Nah," I said. "I'll be fine on the bus." I grabbed my backpack and made my way to the kitchen. David and Amy were pretty good for foster parents. They didn't get in the way much, and the fridge was always full of food. Amy sat at the kitchen table like a block of ice. She nodded to me.

David's voice seemed a bit pitched. "It's the last day of summer school, right?"

"Yeah," I said.

"Well, at least that's over, right?" He chuckled.

"Yeah, though I won't be able to use the school pool for swim practice." I grabbed a wrapped sandwich out of the fridge. "Thanks, Amy."

"You're welcome," she said, eyes fixated on her empty cup.

David opened his mouth like he was going to say something. Amy silenced him with a look.

"See yah," I said and left. It had been a rough week for David. I gave them about a month, then I'd get a new place to park myself. Maybe they could patch things up without me around. I pulled my bus card out of my wallet. The Johnson's lawn needed mowing again. Good thing I still had a few dollars to fill up the gas can. I was only about a dozen lawns away from getting a third-hand car. Then I could move myself instead of standing around, waiting for someone else's bus.

*****

The school bell rang for lunch as the rain poured down. I tried one last time to pop a globe like Mr. Sanderson asked. Fuzzy and yellow again, but he seemed accepting. "Well," he said. "At least you're more consistent."

"Does that mean I pass?"

"Let's switch it up a bit. I want you to try some elemental magic," he said and pulled out a candle.

I rubbed my hands against my legs. "I haven't practiced that in a while."

"Your transcript had it marked as incomplete. I know we didn't get back to it since you joined us, but it's important that you get it right."

Did the transcript mention what happened? "You might want to get—"

"Just cast the spell Cassius," he said, cleaning his glasses.

I focused on the candle wick and skimmed into the magic. My fingertips were warm and gave a small glow.

"Yes. Good," said Mr. Sanderson. "Now snap."

I snapped my fingers, feeling the spell-form fuzz out as I did so. The candle remained unlit.

"Try again, from the beginning."

I waded a little deeper into the magic, reset, and tried again. Nothing.

"Again," he said. "You're holding back, I can sense it. Let it flow through you."

"Mr. Sanderson?" I asked. "Does my transcript mention what happened at my last school?"

He slapped his hand on the table. "Do it again."

I shook my head and dove deep. I focused on the candle, readied my fingertips and, with a nod from Mr. Sanderson, snapped them.

The entire candle roared into flame, twisting and melting as the fire consumed it. Mr. Sanderson jumped back, staring wide-eyed at the rapidly expanding pool of burning wax on his desk. I felt his magic rise and the fire was out; the remains of the candle rimed with frost. He stared at the scorched desk-top for a minute. "I think we're done for today."

"I'm so sorry, Mr. Sanderson," I said.

He waved me off. "It's fine. Just keep practicing; outdoors, preferably. I'll check in with you in a few weeks when I get back from Korea."

"If I don't pass, Coach won't let me on the swim team next year."

"You've made some progress, which is great." He closed his notes up in his briefcase. "Just keep working at it."

*****

With the kitchen locked up for summer, the cafeteria was almost empty. I grabbed a seat near the windows and watched the rain while I ate my sandwich. Coach was sitting a few tables over, trying and failing to get another teacher, a blonde with nice legs, to laugh at something he said.

A blue Camaro pulled into the parking lot, tires squealing and high beams shining in the rain. It came to a halt, perfectly parked. The lights died and Jacob got out. Of course it's him. He strode towards the gym, coming up to the cafeteria window when he saw me. "What's the matter, loser?" he shouted. "Afraid of getting wet?" He laughed, then turned and walked away.

My throat tightened, and I coughed on the last of my sandwich.

"You okay?" called Coach.

I swallowed. "All good, Coach," I said. "I'm heading over now."

"I'll be over in a bit," he said, turning back to the blonde who was rummaging through her purse.

By the time I got over to the pool and changed, Jacob and his swim team buddies were doing laps.

Jacob stopped and hung on a lane line. "Thought you weren't swimming today, loser."

I started my warm up. "You know me, Jacob, born to disappoint you."

"Well," he said. "It's not me you need to worry about disappointing."

Coach was happy with my times. If I let Jacob blow off some steam, could I get some slack? I climbed the starting block of lane eight, which the rest of the team avoided like the plague. "So who should I worry about?"

"Well, let's see," he said, posing with his hand to his chin, the great thinker. "I suppose you don't have to worry about disappointing your parents."

33

My chest froze and I couldn't breathe. I stared at the other end of the pool. Twelve strokes from dive to turn, then fifteen and turn. I forced myself to breathe. Twelve strokes after the dive, then fifteen each lap.

"But what about Elanor?" asked Jacob. "You're keeping her happy, right?"

I got ready on the blocks, keeping my eyes on the wall clock as it counted down to the next minute.

"Oh!" said Jacob, acting shocked. "Trouble in paradise? So soon?" The rest of the team laughed. "What's the matter, can't pry her out of the library?"

"We're not rushing," I said.

"Ah," he said, nodding. "Performance issues." He stuck a finger up in the air, then pointed it down.

I let the minute mark pass and straightened up. "No. We're just not rushing. Besides, I'm more concerned if you're using protection."

Jacob blinked. "What?"

"Well, I've only been here a few months and you're Bethany's sloppy fourths by my count." I gestured to the pool. "If I have to swim in the same water as you, I'd feel better knowing you wrapped it up."

The others were silent, except for Reed. His normal stutter disappeared as he brayed with laughter. Jacob's face turned bright red. He opened his mouth, but the shriek of a whistle silenced him.

"Alright!" called Coach. "First group on the blocks." He pointed at me. "Why aren't you wet yet? This isn't a daycare."

We got set on the blocks, Jacob in his prime spot of lane four, me still in lane eight.

"One hundred meter sprint," shouted Coach. "Show me what you got." He turned to the wall clock and put the whistle to his lips.

"I'm going to kick your ass, loser," said Jacob.

I looked him in the eyes. "Ten bucks says I beat you."

Jacob's smile became a feral grin. "You're on."

"Ready!" called Coach.

The whistle shrieked. I leapt from the blocks and dove into lane eight. I kicked once, twice, turned up and broke the surface with kick three. Twelve strokes, eleven, ten, nine. I couldn't see anyone, and the water was buttery smooth. Three, two, one, touch the wall and turn. Fifteen strokes to go. I hit the chop from my wake and pushed through to calmer water. Seven, six, five. I risked a glance. I was neck and neck with someone a few lanes over. Touch and turn. Fight through the chop. The water was rough, too rough. Five, four, three. Still rough? I reached but had to glide a half-second to touch. Turned, and the chop battered me. My arms and legs burned. I was swimming uphill against the chop and losing. Two. One. Plus one. Plus one. Touch.

My lungs grabbed at the air as I held onto the wall.

"Lane eight suits you," said Jacob. "A losing lane for the loser who just lost ten bucks."

We got out of the water as group two took the blocks. I dove for my magic and fuzzed on some goggles. I watched as the faint trace of an aura in lane eight faded to nothing.

"You freaking cheat," I said.

Jacob stepped close, his finger jabbed into my chest like a dagger. "You take that back or I'm going to take your money and still kick your ass."

"Someone spelled the water." I let go of the goggles, fists clenched. "You that scared of me?"

Jacob snorted. "If you don't have ten bucks to your name, own up." His finger darted forth with each word. "I. Don't. Cheat."

"Is there a problem, Mr. Clayton?"

I looked over at Coach. Bethany was there, smirking, behind him.

"No Coach, no problem." I forced my fists to relax.

The Sending floated into my mind, clear and cold over hollow laughter. Poor Cas. If your mouth wasn't so full of nasty things you could swim faster.

"Good," said Coach. "Because I don't have problems in my swim team, understand?"

I nodded. "Yes Coach."

Bethany settled into the bleachers, her face fierce and eyes locked on me. Group two finished and got out of the water.

"Group one," called Coach. "Ready!"

*****

I walked up the street to David and Amy's house, my arms and legs like burning rubber, my shoes squelching and my wallet ten bucks lighter. I entered through the kitchen door, peeled off my shoes and tried not to make too many puddles on my way to the bathroom.

One hot shower later, I almost felt human. The bed looked so good, but there was a note on the pillow from Amy. *Elanor called, asked if you could meet at 3pm at Barber Park. She sounds nice.* There was a number I didn't know.

Did she move? What's up with the new number? Why call? I can't Send back but she can Send to me, say hi, let me know what's going on.

I stared at the note. Barber Park was less than two miles away, so I could walk there. Wait, three? The clock by the bed showed two-thirty. My legs throbbed to remind me that running was not an option. I'd have to transfer to another bus loop to get there from here, too long. David was at work and Amy was out. I was trapped.

The hell with it. If it was a day to cash the checks my mouth kept writing, then fine.

I used the phone to order a taxi, then jumped into some fresh clothes and out the door. My ride pulled up, I passed him some cash and off we went. Crap. I didn't call to let her know I was coming.

The car stopped. "You okay, kid?"

I looked up at the driver, who was peering at me in his mirror. We were at a red light by the train tracks. "Yeah, I'm okay. I just realized I forgot something."

"You want to go back?"

I took a breath, held it, and let it go. "No thanks. I'll deal with it."

He nodded and focused on the road as the lights changed to green.

I closed my eyes as the taxi drove on. I painted a picture of Elanor in my mind for a Sending link. The magic flowed gentle and smooth. Her shining red hair. Her sparkling brown eyes. Her laugh with that little hiccup in it I loved. The feel of her hand in mine. My fear for her with the ghost. Sadness at the news of her trip away. Joy at the idea of laying next to her, morning sun shining in her hair, the desire to kiss… oh dammit. Did I send all that?

The taxi jerked to a stop, and I was at the park.

Chapter 6

I SAT AT A PICNIC TABLE and watched the clouds roll by. The park was empty except for a couple walking their dog.

My watch said four. Idiot. She called because we were rotten and fell apart, like everything else in my life. She wanted to be decent and tell me in person. Now I've gone and sent... I don't even know what I sent. I should've called and gotten it over with on the phone. She's not coming, she's never going to call, and we're done because I acted like a psycho stalker. What a freaking day.

"Hey Cas!"

Elanor was walking towards me, smiling. Her hair was a cloud around her head instead of its normal ponytail.

"Uh, hi," I said.

She sat down next to me and I was enveloped by the smell of lilacs. I never liked them before, but now they smelled delicious.

"Sorry I'm late," she said. "You didn't call, so I only knew what was going on when you, you know."

"I'm so sorry about that," I said.

She smiled. The dog barked and someone shouted in the distance.

"I uh...."

"I'm sorry," she said.

"You said that."

"No, for not being in touch sooner."

Here it comes. "It's okay," I said.

"No," she said, shaking her head. "The trip with my parents was crazy busy. We ended up doing a few extra days on the road. We were barely in the state when my mother announces that we were going to this spa, just the two of us. They didn't have any sort of phone out there. It was only another two days and I needed some time to process everything, so…."

"Some time," I said. "To sort things out."

"Yes."

"Okay," I said and got up. "Well, I'm glad you got that time."

"Where are you going?"

"I believe this is the part where you say that you like me, but only as a friend?"

She stared at me. Damn those eyes. I'm never going to smell lilacs again and not think of them.

She laughed. "What? No!"

My knees decided they had had enough for today and sat my ass back on the bench.

"Are you okay?"

"Sorry," I said. "I've had a very rough day." I stared at her. "So, you're not breaking up with me?"

She smiled. "No." She brushed the hair back from her face and took a breath. "I needed some time. Some space to think about things. That whole ghost thing was very intense and things, we, happened very quickly after that. I didn't know if I truly felt that way or if it was some type of Stockholm syndrome."

"I, uh… yeah, okay. That makes sense."

"And I guess you feel that way too, from what you sent to me."

My face burned. I looked away, my throat tight. Wait, what? I looked back to see her smiling at me. "You weren't sure how I felt?"

"Well, you're actually pretty good about talking instead of leaving things locked up inside," she said, then frowned. "Which is kinda weird for a guy. A good weird though, in your case."

The sun shone high in the sky and lilacs bloomed around me. My stomach felt... warm.

"I was in my head too much," she said.

"We're not rotten," I said.

She shook her head. "We're not rotten."

I took her hand in mine and felt my chest tremble.

"Well, if it isn't two peas from a haunted pod."

Jacob and Bethany came out from the walking trail, faces flushed. Bethany wiggled her hips and tugged her skirt down.

"So you got her out of the library after all," said Jacob.

"Hey Jacob," said Elanor, rolling her eyes. "I thought that was your car in the parking lot."

"So what are you two up to?" asked Bethany. "Concocting more ghost stories?"

"Nah," I said. "Just hanging out."

"Ooh," smirked Bethany. "Cas and Elanor, sittin' in a tree."

"Won't be no baby though," said Jacob. "Cas is afraid of getting wet."

Bethany's laugh clawed my spine.

Elanor squeezed my hand. "I wouldn't look to forward to having her barefoot and pregnant Jacob. Bethany almost failed Home Ec. I'm not sure she can boil water."

Bethany stepped forward, hands balling into fists. "You little—"

"Not now," said Jacob, grabbing her arm as I stood up. "I got a race tonight."

Bethany broke free of Jacob's grip and glared at him. "Don't do that again." She stepped away, rubbing her wrist.

"Is there something on at the Speedway tonight?" asked Elanor. "I didn't think the other tracks raced on a Friday."

"No," said Jacob, grinning. "It's a street night."

Elanor's eyes widened. "So that's why you have those pro-tires on."

I frowned. "You're doing street races? That's risky."

Jacob shrugged. "Only if you get caught, and I never do."

"Jacob's an excellent driver," said Elanor. "His Camero's almost at stage one spec too."

Jacob leaned closer and dropped his voice. "Not almost, not since last week."

"Wow! Congrats!"

Bethany sniffed. "He blew all his money on it too. Can't even afford a decent dinner for his girlfriend."

"Oh, I got a little bank-roll left," said Jacob. "But that's for my stake tonight." He grinned. "I should clean up nicely with those upgrades."

"You better," said Bethany, grabbing him by the shirt. She kissed him. "And you better get cleaned up before you go. You stink."

"Only of you," he replied.

"And that's too much info," I said.

"Come on Beth," said Jacob. "Let's get some takeout, I'll buy." He looked at me. "After all, I can afford it after my first win today."

Bethany laughed. "Ten bucks won't beat the filet mignon I've got at home." She turned and walked away. "Bye El. Oh, remember to wash your mouth out after you kiss him, your boyfriend talks a lot of shit."

Jacob stopped and glared at me. "What did he say now?"

"Oh, nothing new," said Bethany. "Just that dirty mouth of his from the pool today."

Jacob looked at Bethany, surprise clear on his face. "Who told you about that?"

"What?"

"Who told you about what he said at practice today? Because it wasn't me."

"Oh, I can't remember baby," said Bethany. "Why does it matter?"

"Was it Reed?"

Bethany frowned. "So what if it was? Does it matter who told me? It was nasty, and I got to watch him choke on it."

Jacob stared at Bethany, his face going red, his mouth twisted into a thin line of barbed wire. "It was you," he said. "You spelled the water in lane eight."

She shrugged. "So what? You would've won even without me." She glared at me. "And he deserves it."

Jacob shook his head, his voice cold. "I've told you before not to mess with any race I run, swim or drive." He dug into his pocket and threw a crumpled note on the ground by my feet. "I. Don't. Cheat." He pointed at Bethany. "I will get you home. Then we are done."

"Done?" shouted Bethany. "You're done with me? Over him?"

"It's got nothing to do with him!" Jacob yelled back. "You've got no respect for me, for who I—"

"Respect? You want respect? How about putting your girlfriend first instead of your stupid car."

"At least I know my car isn't getting driven around town by everyone with a stick!"

Bethany screamed and leapt at Jacob, fingers like claws. Jacob grabbed her hands, side-stepped, and let her momentum tumble her to the ground. She sat up, teeth bared, and magic rose in a howl that froze my spine.

Jacob stared in disbelief. "You are crazy!" he said, stumbling back.

I stood up in front of Elanor, the thought of a shield forming in my mind.

"Bethany!" called Elanor. "No! Don't!"

Bethany smacked her hand on the ground and screamed. The magic stopped as she stood up.

"To hell with you!" she yelled at Jacob. "You're going to regret this!" She turned and stomped off. We stared at each other for a moment. Jacob shook his head and left.

My eyes met Elanor's. "Holy crap!" she said.

"That was insane!"

"I can't believe she almost pulled magic on Jacob," said Elanor. "That is crazy!"

"Makes me kinda sorry I cracked that joke today," I said. "Almost."

"I don't know what you said, but honestly it was a matter of time. She has been on a wild streak for months."

I bent down and picked up my ten-dollar bill. Maybe today is turning out okay. "I can't offer filet mignon, but would you like to get some dinner?"

"Yes, please," she said. "But first I have to check in with my new job to see when they want me to start."

"Okay, did you Send for your parents or," I searched in my pockets for loose change. "There should be a pay phone around here somewhere."

She laughed. "No silly, I got my own wheels now."

We walked over to the parking lot. Elanor's new car was a rental-fleet survivor, but the engine rumbled to life without hesitation, and it was freshly cleaned and well-polished.

"Nice ride," I said as we rolled down the street from the park.

"Thanks, it was a present from my dad. You were working on getting a car before I left, how's that going?"

"I'm a few hundred bucks away from something like this," I said. "After it's been in a wreck."

*****

Elanor's new job was on the edge of old downtown, in a two-story brick building that looked every inch the historic monument it was listed as; old, blackened, and looming over you in a way that seemed like it was ready to collapse at any minute. The window shades were down, and I winced at the glare from the late afternoon sun. The faded paint on the front door declared the store's name as "Migina's", above a tableau of a lithe Fae girl holding up a sliver of a moon.

"Looks closed," I said.

"Yeah, the owner is just getting back from a trip." Elanor pulled out a small plastic block from her pocket and flipped it open.

"A cell phone? Was that the new number you called from?"

She laughed. "Yes. I was hoping you would call so I could talk to you from wherever I was."

"Show off," I said with a smile.

"Another daddy present," she said, her mood fading like the sun behind a storm cloud.

"I thought you had a good time on the trip?"

"It's… weird." The lock on the building's front door clicked. "I'll tell you about it later."

A tall, dark-haired man opened the shop's door. Well-groomed, with tinges of gray in his hair, he frowned at us. "I'm sorry, but we're not open for walk-in customers right now."

"Are you Mr Sawyer? My name is Elanor Davis. You've been speaking with my father about me working here this summer?"

His face flipped from irritated to smiles in an instant. "Of course! Come in, come in. Yes, your father sent that you should be by today to fill out the paperwork." He looked at me. "And you are?"

"Cassius," I said. "I'm with her."

He nodded. "Very well, then. Call me Mordecai. Welcome."

The interior of the shop smelled of dust and disinfectant. The flickering lights revealed dusty shelves, filled with cheap trinkets inspired by real Fae craftsmanship. Behind the counter towered an ancient medicine dispensary that was meticulously clean. Gleaming glass bottles and canisters were full of liquids, herbs, sticks and powders.

Mordecai waved Elanor over to the counter. "Here, my dear, a few forms to fill out. Tedious business, government paperwork, but necessary."

Elanor got out her driver's license. "Looks like there's a good bit of set-up to do, when are you planning on opening?"

"It will be a few days yet, I'm afraid." He brushed his hair back, and it fell perfectly into place. He looked at me. "A few shipments have gone astray, but that gives us time to get this place cleaned up and ready."

I picked up an overly eldritch box, stamped with Fae symbols, and blew the dust off it. "When were you last open?"

"Oh, it's been a few years," said Mordecai with a wry smile. "These trinkets do little but take up space and add to the atmosphere. Most of my proper business is mail orders for Fae medicinal supplies, which I run through a warehouse in High Point."

I nodded and replaced the box.

Mordecai left Elanor at the counter, picked up the box and wiped it down with a cloth. "So, how long have you two been dating?"

"Uhh. Well it's been two months, but she was away for a while so we've kinda had to start over."

He nodded. "For what it's worth, there seems to be a powerful bond between you." He put the box down. "I have a knack for sensing that sort of thing."

"Good to know."

"But I admit to being confused. I asked the school to put me in touch with their best, most competent magic student, yet I sense she is as weak as a kitten."

45

My muscles tensed. "El is the best in school with magic." I straightened up and looked directly into his dark eyes. "She's so good that they can't teach her anything else. She's already onto college courses and I bet she'll graduate those before she's twenty."

Mordecai returned my stare. "I find that highly unlikely," he said. His lips tightened in a smile. "Although given how low standards can be in human schools, perhaps you're right." His eyes narrowed. "It is commendable how much you stand up for her. Does she, perhaps, teach you magic?"

"Um, yeah. That's how we met. She had to tutor me when I started at the school."

"Your tutor. In addition to normal classes?"

"Yeah."

"So you are untrainable? Am I dealing with the weak leading the helpless?"

I wanted to punch him in his smug, smiling face. "My own problems are the opposite. I have to dive-up so much power to make anything work that the construct breaks. El is helping me to re-work the spells forms, strengthen them. Something that no school teacher has ever done."

Mordecai nodded and grinned. "Because they don't care about you. Yes, it all fits. Very good." He turned, then looked back at me. "You should try twin-casting. It should help."

"What?"

"Twin casting." He shook his head at my blank stare. "Cast two spells at once. Either the same one twice, or two different ones. Splitting the power flowing from your conduit will make it more manageable. Something anyone with a brain should have been able to tell you years ago."

Elanor walked over, a sheaf of papers in hand. "All done."

Mordecai beamed and took the paperwork. "Wonderful! I'll file all of this in the right spots. I won't need you but half-a-day for the next week as I get things sorted out here with permits and things. Can you start Sunday morning?"

The door opened with a jingle, and in walked trouble. She was tall, taller than me by half a head, with shoulder-length blonde curls framing dark sunglasses. She wore a low-cut white t-shirt with the word 'knockout' on it, tight jeans and high-heeled boots. A sweet cloud of sandalwood and honey perfume cloyed my nose as she sauntered over.

"Victoria," said Mordecai. "I expected to pick you up from the airport."

"Hi Mordecai," she said. "I borrowed a car from my friend, Wayne."

"Victoria, this is Elanor. She's going to be working here at the shop while we get things organized."

"Pleased to meet ya," said Victoria.

"Likewise," said Elanor.

"And who's this?" Victoria tilted her head forward to peek over the tops of her sunglasses. Green eyes looked me up and down. I felt like a piece of meat at the butchers.

"I'm Cassius," I said, clearing my throat.

"My boyfriend," said Elanor, grabbing my hand.

Victoria gave an enormous smile.

"Victoria is visiting for a while to help me with the more tedious errands I have to run. She's on a summer work-exchange program from a high school in Maiakamik."

Elanor's eyes widened. "You're from the Fae lands? Wow, that's—"

"I suppose it is," said Victoria. "Though since I'm from there, it's normal and boring. On the other hand, this place is brand new to me. Perhaps you can tell me all about it or give me a tour sometime?"

"That'd be great," I said. "But right now we have a date to go on."

"Yes," said Mordecai. "And there are some things I need to give you for your stay here, so definitely another time."

"Well, alrighty then," said Victoria. "You guys have a great time!"

The door jingled closed behind us as we returned to the street.

"Someone flunked Drivers Ed," I said, pointing to a white sedan parked in front of Elanor's car, one wheel on the curb and its rear-end half in the road.

Elanor shook her head. "The more I drive, the more I understand why road-rage is a thing. Now, you offered me dinner, right?"

"I did. Still don't have filet mignon money though."

She laughed. "Get in, my favorite diner's not too far away."

Chapter 7

WE SAT IN THE DINER, waiting for our orders. The music playing in the background was stuck on pop songs from a decade ago. The wood table between us, thick with worn varnish, reflected the bare fluorescent bulbs overhead.

"What's wrong?" Elanor asked.

"Hm? Nothing, everything is fine," I said.

"You've been silent since we left the shop. That's not normal."

"I was thinking. By the way, your new boss is an ass, but he told me something that might help with my magic. You ever heard of twin casting?"

She frowned and shook her head. "Two spells at once? No, but that's nothing I could ever do. It might work, but how would you formulate the construct?"

"Yeah, it's a tough one. But more of that, later." I took a breath. "I found out some info about our ghost friend."

Elanor looked surprised, but nodded. "Go on."

"They were the Fergusons. Their twin daughters were Emily and Sarah. We met Emily that night. Everyone thought the fire was an accident until the police realized that Sarah's body was missing."

"Was it ever found?"

"No, and after six months of looking they ran out of leads and the case went cold."

"That's awful. Poor girl."

I nodded. "I promised Emily that night that I would find her sister. And I aim to try."

"I'm in," she said. "Do you have any ideas?"

I let out a breath I didn't realize I was holding. "I'm so happy to hear that. I would've gone on alone, but I'd much rather search for her with you."

We held hands. The server arrived with our food. As we tucked in, Elanor asked, "How did you find that out, anyway?"

"I went to the library."

She paused, burger partway to her mouth. "The library?"

"Yeah. I know how to use the library, and microfilm."

"I'm impressed. The library, microfilm, and you even sometimes pay attention in class." She cracked a smile. "You might graduate after all!"

I stuck my tongue out at her. We both laughed.

"I have a lead," I said after a mouthful of fries. "The newspaper reports mentioned an older case, down in Charlotte, that was similar. Three years before the Fergusons died, Violet and Makasia St. John disappeared. They were also twins. They recovered Violet's body, she drowned in a river. Makasia vanished without a trace."

"Hmm," said Elanor. "Another set of twins, one dead and one missing. It sounds similar, but serial killers nearly always have a pattern in how they kill, not just who. Fire killed the Ferguson's, right?"

"As far as we know," I said.

"It doesn't seem like a strong connection." She shrugged. "Though there may be something there."

"There is something there. Sandra St. John, the mother, claimed that the Fae stole her kids."

"I bet nobody believed her, that's an old wives' tale."

"Yeah, except we met Emily's ghost. And the ward that bound

50

her, from what you said, was most likely Fae work."

Elanor bit her lip and stared at the table. I could almost see her mind turning things over.

"Fae magic and human magic are different," she said after a minute. "The spell constructs are related because they taught us magic, at least according to the old stories. But the metaphysical underpinnings, the philosophy of it, that's unique and quite difficult to understand unless you're steeped in the culture."

"Your boss seemed to be a Fae-supremacist, maybe we should ask him?"

"Are you really bothered by me working there, for him?"

"Nah. Like I said, he's an ass, but you can handle him."

She nodded. "Anyway, some of Fae magic, the ritual side of things, relies upon metaphysical connections to the elements. Natural objects like the sun or the moon. It might make sense, to a Fae, to kill Emily Ferguson with fire after having killed Violet St. John with water."

"So it's possible."

"Yes."

My stomach knotted at the thought. "This might be more than just trying to find out what happened to Emily's sister. Something much bigger is going on, and I aim to find out what that is."

Elanor stared at the table for a moment, then looked me in the eye. "I'm in. All the way."

My stomach relaxed. "Okay. We need to find out more about the case. Track the mother down if we can. I did a quick glance through the phone book but there are bunches of St. John's around Charlotte and none of them listed as Sandra."

"Back to the library then," she said with a smile.

"Your favorite place, I take it?"

"Well," she looked around. "Second favorite."

Her voice sounded full of nostalgia. "You come here a lot?"

"I used to, with my folks." She pushed some fries around on her plate with her fork.

"You okay?"

She took a breath and let it out. "No. I don't know. My parents," she shook her head. "Everything's a mess right now."

I leaned forward and took her hand in mine, watching as something bubbled up inside her.

"I think they're getting a divorce," she blurted out.

Elanor looked so alone. I wanted to tell her how much that sucks, but I doubted I had the words. I held her hand tight and nodded.

She shook her head. "It's funny, in a way. There must have been problems for a while now, but I never saw it. I spent three weeks in a car with them, sharing a hotel room, thinking everything was great. Then I realized that they never spoke to each other. Not one word that wasn't absolutely necessary. Then my mom drags me to that spa for a 'girls only' get away, while dad buys me a car and a cell phone. And when I get home, dad's job has him moving to the Capitol. He's supposed to come back every month, but his office at home is empty. He's 'no longer involved' with local matters."

She grabbed her napkin and held it to her mouth. "Excuse me," she said as she stood and headed to the bathroom.

The server came over with the bill and took our mostly empty plates.

Everything felt numb. I had seen foster parents break up time and time again, but this was different. I tried to drag up any memory of my own parents. The few I had were happy, though tinged with the sadness of never being with them again. I had no clue how to reach out to Elanor and be there for her.

After a few minutes, Elanor came back. "Hey," she said. Her eyes were puffy, but she was smiling.

I tried to plaster a smile on. "Sorry, I was thinking. You okay?"

"Yeah, but we can get out of here? Go someplace else?"

"Sure," I said and grabbed the bill.

We waited by the register. Elanor inspected a book display on the wall, filled with westerns and romance novels. She picked up one with a sweaty, shirtless guy on the front and flipped it over to read the back cover.

"Not that one," I said. "'The Rose Between Thornes' is a much better read."

She looked at me like I had two heads. "And how would you know that?"

The server came, and I paid the bill for our meal. "As an orphan that moves from house to house a lot, you don't get to keep a library. One place last year, I had the choice of three-year-old issues of 'Geomancy Today' or romance novels."

She took my arm as we walked to her car. "That explains a lot about you."

Elanor froze and her eyes glazed over as she received a Sending. That her parents were having problems sucked, but her feeling like I did, feeling alone, made me not alone for the first time in forever. Which was disgusting, but I didn't want to part from her, not yet. "Curfew?" I asked when her eyes cleared.

"No. Not that I would pay attention to that right now." We got in her car. "It was Jacob. He invited us to come to his street race."

My body sagged a bit in the car seat, legs and arms reminding me of my uphill swim practice this morning. The food I'd eaten was trying to send me to la-la-land. "Sounds like fun," I mumbled.

"You look exhausted. Are you sure?"

"Your diner serves a good food coma, but I'll be fine in ten minutes. Let's go."

Chapter 8

I JOLTED AWAKE AS ELANOR TURNED off of the paved road and into the gravel lot of an abandoned gas station. A deep bass line blasted across the lot, threatening to rattle my teeth loose as we pulled up next to a dozen other cars. The sun kissed the tree tops as rain clouds gathered. A small mob danced by the pickup pumping the music and bagged-bottles floated around.

"Wakey-wakey," said Elanor.

"I'm here, I'm here. Where is that again?"

"We're a couple miles outside of town, about a third of the way to Reidsville."

The evening air was hot and muggy. We made our way down the line of cars. Four of them had their hoods popped, showing off their engines, while their owners held court nearby. Jacob's blue Camaro was last on the line, and Jacob was yelling.

"Dammit, Reed! I told you to stay way from her. What are you doing talking about my business behind my back?"

Reed tried to puff up his skinny frame, but he looked ridiculous. "She d... d-eserved to know what he said about her. It wasn't right."

Jacob shook his head. "He wasn't wrong either. I was her fourth since Christmas. You looking to be number five? Go right ahead. I'm done with that."

"Since when?"

"Since today. And when she dumps you in a week for someone else, it'll be your own damn fault."

Reed took a step forward, hands balled into fists, but hesitated when he saw me.

"You better put those little things away," growled Jacob. "And try not to be stupid about this. Bethany wouldn't go for you, not even to piss me off."

Reed pointed his finger at Jacob. "You d… d… you know nothing about me an' her!"

"There is nothing about you and her. Now get out of here. If I see your face again before school starts, I'm going to use to it to wipe my ass."

Reed bared his teeth, then stalked away, cursing.

"It's easy to see why you're the leader of the swim team," I said. "Such a winning personality."

"You don't like it orphan?" asked Jacob. "That's your problem. Because winning is what I do." He walked over to his car, waving for Elanor to join him. "Come on El, have a look at this beauty."

Elanor looked at me.

"Go on," I said, giving her hand a squeeze. "I know you want to."

Smoke drifted about, tinged with the faint scent of weed and cloves. The music dropped out to a whisper as a guy with lanky black hair stood on the bed of the music truck and started shouting, calling everyone over to place bets. The scent of sandalwood and honey washed over me. "Hi there," whispered a voice.

I spun about. Bright green eyes stared into mine, wreathed in blonde curls that almost tickled my nose. I stepped back. "Hey! Victoria," I said. "Hey. What are you doing here?"

"Oh, I heard about a little get-together in the back-country for some racing. Thought it would be fun."

"You sure seem to know your way around for your first trip to Greensboro."

"I work fast and I'm not afraid to ask for what I want," she said. She reached out and walked two fingers up my chest, her nails sharp through my shirt. She bent forward to bring her face close to mine again. "And in a few days, I'm gone and never coming back, so…" she glanced down. My eyes flicked down in response and I was staring down her shirt at round, smooth skin.

My pulse raced, and my temperature spiked. She is intense and I am in deep trouble. I turned away and took a deep, shuddering breath. "I, I thank you but—"

"You would thank me," she said and smiled. "It's sweet, you being loyal." She glanced over to the car line, where Elanor was staring at us. "Misguided, but sweet."

"Loyalty matters," I said.

She shook her head. "If there's something that you want, you make it happen. Waiting for someone to give it to you leaves you buried in the dirt, alone." She strode away, waving to Elanor. "Hi there!"

I took a moment to catch my breath and calm down. By the time I walked over, Victoria was flirting hard with Jacob, hanging on his arm and making moon-calf eyes. Jacob ate it up like a lion served a roast dinner. The driver of a yellow two-door came over to shake hands with Jacob. Elanor excused herself and stalked back to her car with me in tow. The pit of my stomach twisted into knots. Did she think something had happened between me and Victoria?

Behind the steering wheel, she shook her head. "That girl is getting on my nerves."

"I have no idea how she knew about this."

The ice melted from Elanor's spine. "Oh Cas, I'm not mad at you. Her attitude sets me on edge." She started the engine. Several cars were pulling out of the lot, headlights flashing on to pierce the growing darkness.

"Is that it? I thought there was a race tonight?"

"No, it's about to start." We pulled back onto the tarmac behind the music truck and followed the line of cars. "The finish line is in town, at Delwood's drive-in. There are four cars tonight, so they'll run in pairs. Best overall time wins the pot." She floored the accelerator; the car surged as she overtook the music truck before sliding us smoothly back in our lane. "Jacob says there's two grand on the hook tonight."

"You think he has a chance?"

"He's a skillful driver, and those upgrades in his car are sweet. He's got a good chance."

The stomach knot was still there. Jacob was available now. Was she thinking about his car, or him? "So how did you get to become such a gearhead? Was it Jacob?"

She laughed. "Oh no, not him. I mean, he's not stupid, but he's just buying stuff from a magazine."

"So where then?"

"When I was being tutored. There was this guy, Greg. He was a gearhead, and super hot. I was what, twelve? So I thought if I learned enough to impress him, the super-hot twenty-year-old might notice me."

"And did he?"

"Cas!"

"What? You're awesome at lots of stuff. Nothing would surprise me when it comes to you learning things."

"Thank you, but no. The hot twenty-something did not hit on twelve-year-old me. But after he finished teaching me what he could, I found that I still enjoyed figuring out how things worked and fit together. When I took that to magic, started treating it like a science, is when I figured out how to make the most of what I have."

"Wait. How many tutors did you have?"

"A new one every few months it felt like. They overlapped, so it's a bit of a blur. Most were specialists in some arcane sub-field who only came in to teach me one thing. But all the bits and pieces fit together, so now I can cast like a normal person."

The knot in my stomach relaxed. She may have had a family, but they upended her life as much as mine was without one. "You're not normal. You're better than that."

"You sure? I can get pretty weird." She tried to blow away a wisp of her hair that had gotten free from her ponytail.

"Doesn't matter. You're my kind of weird."

We entered Greensboro and came off the highway to the city roads. Sure enough, right in front of us was the drive-in restaurant. As we parked, I tucked the loose strand of her hair behind her ear. She leaned her head against my hand, the touch of her cheek electric against my palm. We leaned close, breathing in sync, staring into each other's eyes.

"Hey y'all, welcome to Delwood's." The server leaned against the car and shoved menus at us. "I know it's a drive-in, but people eat here. You want anything else, better go find a room, ya hear?"

"Yes mam," we chorused, grinning.

Elanor's eyes glazed briefly. "They've started. Come on."

We got out and joined the crowd looking up the street. I peered through the blinding orange glare of the streetlights. The road was empty except for a white sedan pulling into the gravel lot across the intersection. Magic stirred around me. Oh, yeah. I tried to enhance my eyesight; nothing but fuzz. By the time I saw what was happening, everything would be over. A girl laughed unabashedly. Victoria? No. It was another blonde, sitting on the bed of the music truck. The bookie was standing up in the truck bed, his eyes squarely on the road.

Okay. Twin casting. Two spells at once. That's like… butterfly stroke. Both hands hitting the water at the same time. I closed my eyes, dove into the magic, and formed twin sets of spell goggles. The spells formed clean and clear.

Is this what normal spell casting feels like? This easy?

My eyes swam and blurred. Reflexively, I had tried to put both of them on at once. Idiot. I could feel the spells in my mind like I was running my fingers over them, understanding their shape, feeling them flex and move. I used one spell to enhance my vision. The orange glare of the streetlights disappeared. I could see as if it were a clear day and when I focused on the distant off-ramp, like a zoom lens. I rolled the other spell around with my mind, pushed on it like a rubber Frisbee, inverting it. I was floating. The second felt like it could fit into the first. If one enhanced my eyes this much, what would two do? I melded them together.

Bright colors sprang from everywhere. Rainbow swirls surrounded everyone. Something cerulean floated between everything and everyone, concentrating on their eyes. Magic? Was that actually magic?

Elanor was holding on to my arm but staring down the street. "I felt you do something. Can you see alright?"

"I can see. Everything." Elanor was golden. The crowd was a vibrant, vibrating rainbow.

"Here they come! Jacob's in the lead!"

The crowd roared. Jacob's blue car weaved back and forth as he came down the ramp, his yellow competitor drafting, trying to slingshot around him. They were a mile away and I could feel the engines roaring through the blood pounding in my ears, my eyes throbbing with adrenaline, head exploding. Too much! I broke the connection, my chest sucking down air.

In the middle of the road stood a giant of darkness and fire. Magic whirled around it and all the rainbows grayed. A pit of dread cleaved my stomach. The giant reached forward and smashed into Jacob's car while it was in mid-swerve. A putrid green shock wave flashed over everything. Jacob's tires screeched as the car failed to straighten up. Sliding sideways, it clipped a street light. The car fishtailed, flipping into the air end over end.

Everyone was screaming. Elanor's hands clamped on my arm, her weight dragging me down as she collapsed. Jacob's car smashed down on its roof, slid, then crashed over on its side to a stop as it hit the sidewalk by the drive-in.

The giant vanished. A cerulean web flashed from the car and into the distance like a bolt of lightning.

I held Elanor tight as she sobbed into my chest. My body locked up. The world was a miasma of muddy colors and I was drowning in oil. Sirens crashed into my ears and I dropped the spell, returning the world to its true state of darkness.

"Help is on the way," I said as tears rolled down my face.

"It's too late," she sobbed. "Too late."

Chapter 9

THE EARLY MORNING SUN STUNG my eyes. My body ached like I was half-way through a bad cold. I groaned and got out of bed. The memories of last night flooded back. Jacob's car flipping. The chaos of the police and the ambulance. The shock and crying of the crowd washing over me before I could drop the spell that helped me to see and feel more than I ever had before.

That spell must have let me see the ghost that killed Jacob. Everyone else thought he lost control, wiped out. His death a tragic accident, not brutal, deliberate murder. Was it Emily? Had she escaped the house of her death after all? But why kill Jacob? Why then? Was it something I did? Did the twin casting empower her somehow?

My heart longed to be with Elanor. Her mom had collected her from the drive-in, which was better than getting dropped home by the cops, I suppose. David and Amy were not impressed. I could still feel Elanor shaking in my arms and all I wanted to do was hold her. Whatever I'm feeling, she has got to be ten times worse. I've only known ass-Jacob for a few months. She knew decent-Jacob for years. And now dead-Jacob might be my fault.

I headed to the kitchen for some food and found David folding up the sleeper-couch in the living room.

"Morning," he said. "How are you feeling?"

"Like I got worked over by a baseball bat. Did you sleep out here?"

David picked up the cushions off the floor and put them on the couch. "Yeah, it was for the best."

"Was it because of me? Because of the cops and the accident?"

He shook his head. "No. We decided this long before you came home."

I nodded, took a step to the kitchen, then stopped as a band tightened around my heart. I turned back to David. "I'd say it's none of my business, but I've gotten used to being here. Last night ended… horribly." I took a deep breath. "But before that happened, it was the best day of my life. Today is going to suck. Tomorrow, too. But after that, I may actually have a real chance, for the first time in my life since my parents died, to be happy, because I've met someone and we're solid."

"This Elanor girl."

"Yeah. She's amazing. I don't think I let myself notice her when she tutored me because I was expecting everything to end, and me to move on to another home, another school. But I don't want that now. Even if I have to fight… whatever. I won't lose her."

David's eyes stared at me, but his mind was clearly somewhere else.

"If nothing else, last night taught me that if you don't act to make something happen, you get buried in the dirt, alone." Despair washed over me at the thought of being without Elanor, but then determination kicked its ass. "I don't know what's going on between you two, but I'm asking you to fix it. I need you to fix it."

David nodded. "Done."

I left him by the couch and grabbed some breakfast. The fog in my head was lifting. I had to do something, but what? I wanted to swim, but the school was closed and the Y would only deplete what little funds I had left. I needed to call Elanor, to hear her voice. But no, she needed whatever sleep she could get and besides, what would I say to her? The ghost I want to help killed your friend? My leg was jack-hammering under the kitchen table. I grabbed my things and walked out.

When I got to the corner, the bus was almost there. I needed to keep moving, so I caught it and headed into town. The thought of the ghost, filled with rage, smashing into Jacob's car, kept playing in my head. The flash of green that made me want to vomit. And what was that spell that fired off at the end? I blinked as the bus came to a stop and realized I was in downtown. I hopped off and headed to Migina's. Mordecai might have an insight, but can I tell him what I saw? I didn't know, but it was a place to go and my legs needed to walk somewhere.

The window shades were still down, though a new sign in the door announced that it would open 'soon'. Right. Now what? A muffled thump followed by vigorous cursing came from the alleyway. It was Mordecai, struggling with a large box upended on the pavement.

"Hey there, you need a hand?"

"Cassius." Mordecai stood up and wheezed, his hand pressed against his side. "Elanor's not in today."

"I know." I righted the box and picked it up. It was heavy, but not that bad. "I was hoping to see you, actually."

He waved me in through the alley door into the back room of the shop, which included a kitchen. "There, on the table is fine, thank you." He sat down on a chair and used a handkerchief to pat the sweat from his head.

"Are you okay? You look a bit gray."

"I'm fine, thank you. I get like this from time to time. I'll be fine once the stress of getting this shop open has passed."

I grabbed him a glass of water and sat at the table. He took a sip, then nodded his appreciation.

"I wanted to say thank you," I said. "I tried that twin-casting trick you talked about."

"Oh? How did it go?"

"Amazing! It came so easily it was like breathing."

"Really? Just like that?"

"Yeah," I stood up and began pacing. "It was like. Well, when I swim, when I do the butterfly stroke. Both hands have to hit the water at the same time. I did that, and it worked."

"Well, I'm glad for you. That's a difficult technique. You must have quite a lot of power if it came that easily."

I shrugged. "All I know is that for the first time, I felt what it must be like to be a normal person who whips up a spell when they need it."

"And I can see what the means to you," he said. "You should have a specialist teacher helping you, someone who can give you a proper education. Your talent is being wasted here."

"Well, I have Elanor." I remembered holding her against the chaos of last night. "She's amazing."

"I can see that," Mordecai said. "You know, there are exchange programs to schools in Maiakamik, if you have a sponsor. The schools there could help you."

"You'd do that for me? Why?"

Mordecai smiled. "I hate to see talent wasted, and I think yours might be quite special."

I swallowed. "That's not… unattractive. But it would mean leaving Elanor. So, thank you, but no."

"Well, the offer's open if you change your mind." He patted the box on the table. "Now, would you mind helping me to put this on the main counter so I can unpack it?"

"Sure." The box clunked as we moved to the sales floor. "What's in this? Rocks?"

"More or less." Mordecai opened it and pulled out a small bag of plastic beads that rattled.

"Oh, rave rocks."

Mordecai laughed. "Is that what they call them these days?"

"They have a loop attached to them, right? So you can put a braid through and wear them in your hair?"

"Yes. Give them ten minutes, channel a little magic and they glow." Mordecai inspected the bag. "Ah, I see why they're called 'rave' rocks. The plastic shells are all different colors."

"That's Babingtonite in there, right?"

Mordecai looked surprised. "Yes. Well, not pure Babingtonite. They're clear quartz crystals with traces of the mineral. It's the interaction that allows the glow. You seem to be full of surprises today."

"You know in doctor's offices there's always these old, boring magazines? Well, for a while I lived with a guy who collected them."

Mordecai laughed.

The thought of Emily reaching out to murder Jacob drifted through my mind. My eyes widened as a shot of adrenaline hit my brain. "It glows because the magic reinforces the aura of the owner, right? Couldn't you use that to reach out to the owner?"

"Not with these, the mineral content is too low and it's too small. For something like that…" he opened up a drawer in the apothecary and took out a small box. Inside was a stone, black with white speckles, about the size of an egg. It was nestled inside a metal framework wrought with small clear crystals. "This is a 'touch-stone'. The Fae used these until about a century ago when they fell out of fashion. It's big enough that when you charge it with your aura, there's enough of an imprint that someone could use it to Send to you, even if they hadn't met you."

He put it in my hand. It was cool to the touch and heavier that I thought it would be.

"The proper nobility of the day would have customized cages, so you'd know who had dropped by while you were out, or had a special message for you. The white stones are quartz. So, like your rave rocks, the whole thing will glow if the original owner channeled magic, as a means of authentication."

"The cage, that's like a Faraday cage, right? So the aura lasts longer?"

"Exactly. And to stop it from being contaminated by other auras."

The ghost from last night hovered in my mind. It might be the only way to track it down, if there's anything left to trace. "How much?"

"It's priced at two hundred. Babingtonite in that size and purity is rare." He shrugged. "It's also been sitting in a drawer from before this shop was closed a decade ago. Keep it, as a token of our friendship."

"Thanks!" I slipped the caged touch-stone into my pocket. Maybe this guy wasn't so bad. "Oh, so you know. If Elanor comes in tomorrow, she may be a bit out of it."

Mordecai's eyes narrowed. "If? I thought she and I had an agreement."

"You do," I said. "Did you hear about the accident last night?"

"Yes, a most regrettable event." He frowned. "Did you know him?"

"Only a few months. He was captain of the swim team at school. I've been practicing with them, trying to get on the team next semester. Elanor knew him for years though, so she's pretty upset."

Mordecai nodded. "Yet you knew him enough to spend time with him? Go to parties, drink beer in the woods, that type of thing?"

Something about his tone was weird. "We didn't hang out like that, no."

He leaned forward, dark eyes staring into mine. "But

something connected you, recently. Otherwise you wouldn't be as upset as you are."

My stomach churned. The metallic crunch of Jacob's car flipping echoed in my ears. "I was there last night… when he died. So was Elanor. I haven't spoken to her today, but it really tore her up last night."

Mordecai nodded. "Well, I promise to be assiduous with her when she arrives." He sighed and looked at the box of rave rocks. "Now, if you'll excuse me, I have work to do."

*****

Back on the street and it wasn't even noon yet. My legs had calmed down, but I was light-headed. Time for a bite, but none of the downtown restaurants were open and I had at least a twenty-minute wait for the next bus somewhere else. The only place within a short walk was… the drive-in from last night. My stomach clenched and my mouth dried up. My fingers closed around the touch-stone in my pocket.

"Fine," I said. "Let's get this done." I started walking. The smell of lilacs surrounded me. Elanor was Sending to me. If I twin-cast to receive, would I get an echo? Best to try a globe and the receiving spell, if that would even work. The real world fuzzed, but I could see Elanor in front of me.

"Hey you," she said and smiled. I could not only see the smile, but feel her emotion behind it like the sun.

"Hi—" My head exploded with pain. Dammit!

"Are you okay? What happened?"

My cheeks were on fire. "Street lamp," I said, holding onto the offending pole as I rubbed my forehead. "Jumped out and hit me in the face."

Elanor laughed. "I was about to compliment you on how good your connection was. Should I warn you about the dangers of walking and talking?"

"Thanks, I think I got the lesson on my own."

"Hey, where are you? I tried calling, but your foster parents said you were out." My stomach rumbled and Elanor frowned. "Don't be sharing your hunger with me, I just ate."

"I'm downtown. I stopped by and talked with your boss."

"What about?"

"Mostly to thank him about the twin-casting thing. I've got a small globe running, which is why this connection is so good." My chest tightened. "I also let him know about last night, and that you might not be in such a good spot."

"Oh."

"I'm sorry. That wasn't mine to say, but I didn't want him yelling at you."

"No, it's okay. I was thinking about last night."

"How are you doing?"

"Horrible, but better this morning. Mom is about to give me a ride back there to pick up my car. I know it'll all be cleared up but…"

"Yeah. I know. Look, I was actually heading over there because, well." I paused as my stomach protested being empty. Elanor laughed. "So maybe I'll see you there?"

"Yes. See you soon." She smiled. A wave of warm emotion rolled over me like the perfect bath. Then she was gone.

I blinked and leaned against the rough surface of the light pole. The heat of the summer sun was cold against the shadow of Elanor's touch. Was this, love?

Chapter 10

TWENTY MINUTES LATER I STOOD on the sidewalk up the street from the drive-in, where the ghost stood in the road and killed Jacob as he drove. The crash site was festooned with yellow police tape and frosted with shattered glass. Two people in plain clothes were walking around, taking photographs, while a uniform watched, bored, from the sidewalk. But this was where the murder happened.

I dove into the magic and twin-popped the eyesight enhancement. It took me a while, but I inverted one copy and melded them together. The world around me was colorful, but muted. There, in the road. The colors grayed out and swirled into an oily morass. That was where the ghost stood.

The aura was fading as I watched. The street light for the highway off-ramp changed to red, and the road cleared. I took the touch-stone from its cage and, walking into the road, set it down in the center of the murder residue. I watched as the black stone soaked up the brown aura. A line of traffic stacked up at the intersection, then the light changed. The touch-stone looked coated in oil. I scooped it up and dashed back to the sidewalk as cars raced past me, horns blaring.

The stone felt... wrong. A shiver walked up my arm as I held it up. I could taste rotten ham in the back of my throat. Retching, I stuffed the rock back into its cage. Almost instantly, the sensations disappeared. I dropped the spell, and the world went back to normal.

"Well, at least that worked."

As I straightened up, Elanor drove into the gravel lot.

"What the hell were you doing? You could have been killed!"

I raised my hands as she got out of the car and stalked over. "Yeah, that seemed stupid, but I have a good reason, I swear."

Elanor crossed her arms and raised her eyebrows. "Well? Why is playing in traffic your new favorite past-time? Did you hit your head that hard?"

I held out the caged rock. "It's a touch-stone. It collects and stores aura signatures."

She glared at the stone, then shrugged. "There's nothing," she said.

"Take it out of the cage."

The miasma returned the moment she removed it. Sickening, but not as bad without the sensing spell. Elanor gasped and shoved the stone back into its cage.

"Oh my god! What is that?"

"What do you think it is?"

Elanor frowned. "Is that…"

"Feels a lot like an angry ghost, doesn't it?"

"Okay, what's going on? What aren't you telling me?"

"I think Emily killed Jacob."

Elanor stared at me like I had an extra head that spoke French.

"Last night, before… we were trying to see down the street, right? I couldn't get the eye enhancement to work, so I tried that twin-casting trick Mordecai told me about. And it worked, more than I thought was possible."

"You said, you said you could see everything."

"Yeah. I did something to the spell, I didn't even know I could do it, and I could see auras. Yours, the crowds, and everywhere was this blue mist that I think is magic. When I looked at the

70

cars, it was like I could feel them, like they were alive." I took a breath. "And then I saw Emily. Standing in the road, ten feet tall and full of fire and smoke. She did… something. There was this green flash, and it was only after that, that Jacob's car wrecked."

Elanor stared at the street, then at the caged rock. "So you used this to get a sample of the ghost's aura."

"Yeah. I know it sounds crazy, but I didn't even know if what I saw was real. I had to see if there was any proof. Nobody saw it but me, and with all the pain of Jacob…" my voice caught in my throat. "Of him dying, I didn't want to add to whatever hell you were going through if I didn't have to."

Elanor nodded. "I get it, but there's one problem. This isn't Emily."

"What?"

She handed the touch-stone back to me. "I know it was two months ago, but I got real close and personal with Emily. First, when I caged her, and then when I trapped her in the doll. I believe that you saw a ghost. Whatever you got a trace of, it's evil. But it's not Emily."

My body froze. I swallowed, my mouth dry. "You're sure? There's another pissed off ghost killing people?" Elanor nodded. "Did we start something when we freed Emily? Open some sort of gateway?"

"I don't know, but those cops have been looking at you funny for the past five minutes. Let's get out of here."

I nodded. As I walked around the car to the passenger side, something crushed under my foot. It was an empty wire cage, studded with quartz crystals. Around it were fragments of a black stone, speckled with white.

*****

The sun was approaching its high-point, and the heat of the day had driven everyone out of Barber Park apart from us and the cicadas.

71

Elanor paced in front of me. "Okay, so from what you said, the ghost attacked Jacob. There was a big green flash. His car wrecked. The ghost disappeared and some massive spell went off, right?"

The picnic table shifted as I adjusted my seat. "Yeah, pretty much."

"There weren't a lot of cops at the crash site, and they weren't anywhere close to where you got the aura sample. That means the cops don't suspect a magical cause for the accident or Jacob's death."

"Which makes sense. The only reason we know about it is because of this... thing I'm doing with an eye enhancement spell." I looked down at the touch-stone on the picnic table. "That's the only way I could see the residue in the road. It may be the same for any residue of whatever happened, well—"

"When Jacob died."

"Yeah, sorry."

She held my hand. "I appreciate you trying to be sensitive, I do. And," she said as tears welled in her eyes. "I have cried a lot and will cry a lot more. Right now, I am trying to focus and be present to the facts. So don't be afraid to say it straight, okay?"

"Okay," I said and pulled her close. We held on to each other, breathing in sync, the smell of her hair comforting me. I took a deep breath and let her go. "So. My inverting of the enhancement spell must be what is allowing me to see these things. Whoever is casting the spells must do the same sort of inversion in order to hide them."

"From what I know of how magic works, that's impossible. But it fits all the other impossible things that have been going on, so no matter how strange that is, it has to be true."

On the picnic table, next to the touch-stone, sat the broken metal cage and the fragments we found at the gravel lot. "There is no way this stuff is a coincidence. Touch-stones gather enough aura to allow for a Sending, which means you can also track the aura. I don't know whether this was used to track Jacob or summon the ghost, but someone used it and destroyed the evidence."

Elanor nodded. "Someone who could invert a series of powerful spells, so that the cops are stumbling around with no clue."

"Someone who might be connected to an inverted ward, that hid and sustained a ghost for over a decade."

"And who may well have drowned another young girl and kidnapped her sister a few years before that."

I swallowed, my throat tight. "We're looking for a Fae serial killer."

Her voice trembled. "And we're the only ones who know to look."

She snuggled in close, and I wrapped my arms around her. I clasped my hands tight to keep them from shaking as my heart raced. A Fae serial killer? Someone with decades, perhaps centuries of life, of skill and knowledge behind them, reaching out and murdering children at whim. Invisible, unknowable, but now traceable.

"We could try to trace the ghost," I whispered into her hair. "Though that scares the crap out of me."

"Me too. I can't do that, not now." She stepped back and re-did her ponytail. "What I can do is try to understand this inversion thing. Can you do it again? While I'm linked?"

"Sure." I dove into the magic and twin-cast the eye enhancement. "It's getting pretty easy, thanks to Mordecai."

"Okay," she said as her magic meshed with mine. "Go ahead."

I inverted one spell, trying to comprehend what my magic was doing intuitively, then merged them. Elanor's teeth gripped her bottom lip as she concentrated on what I was doing.

"Okay," she said. "I couldn't see how you did that, but I can see the final form and it kinda makes sense." My magic flowed like a gentle current. Elanor's spell collapsed a few times before it solidified, a twin of what I had done. "Got it!"

We goggled up. Bright colors flowed around us. Elanor gasped, her golden aura shading to blue.

"Oh my god. This is amazing!"

On the picnic table, the caged touch-stone looked like a grease spot on a silk shirt. The current of magic spiked and tugged. Elanor's aura was graying out. She wobbled and grabbed my arm.

"Drop it," I said. "It's too much for you. Drop it!"

We let the spells go and sat together, her body trembling. "Okay, that was too much."

"Let me drive you home."

"And be without my car again? No thanks," she said and smiled. "You can drive me to your home; I'll be fine by then."

*****

David and Amy's house, a single-story ranch-style home, was one of a dozen identical units on the tree-lined cul-de-sac. The large oak tree on the front yard cast a dappled shadow over us as I parked.

We got out of the car. Elanor had been silent while I drove. Once, tears rolled down her face, but she wiped them away before I could say anything.

I gave her one last hug and kissed her hand as she stepped away. "Call me when you get home," I said. "I'm worried about you."

She nodded, her face cloudy, then got in her car and drove off. Walking up to the house, Amy opened the door for me.

"Welcome back," she said. "Was that Elanor?"

"Yeah."

"She's beautiful," she touched my arm as I brushed past her into the house. "You treat her right now, you hear?"

74

"Yes mam."

"Good. Oh, the school called. The swim team is holding a memorial service for the Smith boy tomorrow morning. The details are on the fridge in case you want to go."

"Thanks," I said. Jacob was an ass, but the weight of his death hung on me. "Yeah, I think I will."

Amy smiled, the first one I had seen from her in days. As I walked through to the kitchen, she sat down on the couch next to David to watch TV and put her hand on his knee. David gave me a thumb's up, which I returned. Good. At least someone's making progress.

Chapter 11

THE MILLING CROWD FILLED THE DECK around the school pool, and it was slow-going to walk without knocking someone in.

Hugging, crying teens held whispered conversations, sharing stories. As I walked, I heard about a Jacob I never knew. I had nothing to share, nothing that would do anything but dampen his memory. So I kept moving from group to group until the scent of sandalwood and honey, tinted with lilacs, stopped me.

"Victoria?"

"Hey Cas." She squeezed a crying girl's arm, then turned to me.

"What are you doing here?"

"I'm here to support Jacob's friends."

My eyes widened, and my jaw dropped open. "That's, very kind of you."

She smiled weakly. "Look, I know I only met the guy for, like, five minutes. But I was there, watching when he died. It impacted me too." She looked around at the crowd. "I've recently experienced the loss of a friend, of family. I thought I could help."

My heart burned with shame, and my face flushed. "I'm sorry, you're right. I'm just surprised to see you here, of all places. How did you even know about this?"

"Oh, through the grapevine. I met a few people the other night at the race and, well, they passed the word on."

"Well, thank you for coming."

"Of course," she said. "Were you close with Jacob?"

"No," I said. "I only joined the school a few months ago. I practiced with the swim team, but outside of that he and I didn't move in the same circles."

"No swim team drinking binges in the woods kind of thing?"

My heart stopped for a second, but her face was open and kind. "I never got to drink a beer with him, no."

She nodded. "It was pretty obvious you had some sort of history though, was it Elanor?"

"Look, I appreciate you trying to help—"

"I'm sorry. I'm not trying to get all up in your business. Everyone else is sharing, so I was giving you an opening if you wanted it."

My stomach knotted. "Thanks," I said. The exterior door banged, and I stared in that direction as voices rose.

"Your coach gave an impressive speech..."

The crowd thinned. Bethany stumbled forward, skin gray, eyes red, clothes disheveled. "What are y'all assholes even doing here?" she shouted. "You didn't know him. Not like I knew him. I loved him! And he loved me." She weaved her way towards the pool edge. Reed stepped out of the crowd, arms out. She looked right through him, but turned away from the pool and headed towards me. "And you. Orphan! You have no right to be here." She stopped in front of me, the vodka fumes making me want to gag.

"B...b-ethany," said Reed, stepping forward.

"Oh shut up Reed," she snapped. "If you weren't always sniffing around, pretending to be such good buddies with Jacob, he'd still be alive!"

Reed's mouth twisted and his Adam's apple bobbed up and down. He reached out to Bethany.

"Don't touch me turkey-neck!" Bethany whirled around and shoved him. "Go gobble at someone else."

Reed stepped back, his face reddening, jaw clenched. He turned and stalked off, wiping at his face.

Victoria squeezed my arm. "I think I better go see to him," she whispered, then walked after Reed.

The crowd was thinning out, following Reed's example. Bethany slumped at the edge of the pool against lane four's dive block, staring at the water.

"Not supposed to be this way," she moaned.

I squatted next to her. "Jacob and I knocked heads, but for what it's worth, I respected him for being himself."

Bethany glowered at me, but it was the truth. After a long moment, she looked away. "Yeah," she said. "He never hid who he was." She laughed. "He still doesn't."

"What do you mean?"

"He comes to me, in my dreams. Holds me. Loves me." Tears ran down her face and she touched her chest. "I can feel him, in here, all the time."

One of Bethany's friends from the cheerleader squad knelt next to us and held out her hand. Bethany nodded, and we helped her up. As they walked away, she stopped and turned back to me.

"I never hated you, ya know Cas? You were just a way to get to Elanor."

"Why? What happened between you two?"

"When my mother and I moved here, I was the best student in the class. Everyone loved me. I worked hard, became cheer captain, honors, you name it. Then she came back. In a week, everyone had forgotten about me. She was the prodigy, the amazing one. Because she was so damned weak and yet better than anyone else." Bethany took a step forward and stumbled. "She was even working on taking my Jacob away from me. I know. I know what was going on. She's going to ditch you and break your stupid little heart. She..." Bethany started sobbing.

Coach walked over. "Go on, Monique," he said. "Get her home." He looked at me. "You okay, son?"

"Yeah, she's... upset."

"It's been a crappy day for everyone, and that was before my speech." He frowned. "It sounds like you and Elanor are still together, is that right? I remember you two moon-faced over each other at the end of school. Where is she? I would have thought she'd be here today."

"She didn't want to come. She's grieved at home since Friday night. She's still upset, but she wanted to focus on her new job for a bit to get her life back under control."

Coach nodded. "Makes sense. Funny that she's working on a Sunday though, where's her job at?"

"She's at that Fae curio shop, Migina's, in downtown."

"Really? That place has been closed for a decade."

"Yeah, but they're re-opening in a few weeks and the guy who owns it, Mordecai, needed the extra hand to get everything ready."

"Huh," he said, rubbing his shoulder. "I used to get a tonic from there, helped me to heal up after a rough work-out. Bitter something. It worked but lived up to its name. Tasted absolutely awful." He looked around. Everyone had gone. "You need a lift?"

"That would be great, thanks."

"No problem, just help me lock up."

Chapter 12

COACH SLAMMED ON THE BRAKES and his truck screeched to a stop. Braced as I was against the grab-bar, my chest still jerked tight against the seat-belt.

"There you are, school to girl in five minutes flat." Coach's voice was gleeful. My stomach wasn't sure if the pancakes I had for breakfast were safe or needed to evacuate. "You ever need an advanced driver's lesson, you let me know, ya hear?"

I got out of the truck. "Thanks Coach. Will do."

He laughed, turned up the radio, and drove off in a screech of tires.

The store's front door and window shades were closed-up, but the side-entrance in the alley was open. I was about to call out at the doorway to the kitchenette when raised voices floated through from the shop floor. I sneaked in and peered through the doorway.

Mordecai stood by the counter, a sheaf of paperwork in his hands, as a blonde woman spoke.

"Yes, but this is the third shipment in as many months where it's been blatantly short," she said.

"I assure you, Abigail, I will get to the bottom of it."

"I would check on your staff. They must be stealing it."

"I will. Now, thank you for your help with this," said Mordecai, holding up the papers. "The closing will take place tomorrow?"

"Yes. It'll take a few days to go through land registration, but as of two o'clock tomorrow you will own the property."

"Thank you. I'll wire your fee after the close."

They shook hands. As quiet as I could, I hustled back to the alley door. I knocked loudly and called out. "Mordecai? Elanor? Can I come in?"

Mordecai and the blonde came through from the shop. "Good afternoon, Cassius," he said. "Elanor's upstairs, bringing down some old stock. She won't be long." He waved me through.

"You know Elanor?" the blonde asked.

"She's my girlfriend," I said. The word fell out of my mouth so matter-of-fact. It was concrete. Real. I wanted to say it again and again.

"Wonderful! She's such a nice young lady. Do you go to the same school?"

"Yes, mam."

"So you must know my daughter, Bethany."

Oh crap. "Yeah. I saw her a little while ago at the memorial."

"She's holding up so well. It was a terrible blow, but I'm so proud of her."

I nodded. Was this woman for real? "I'm sorry, but I need to…"

"Of course, of course," she said.

I walked away while Mordecai and Bethany's mom exchanged another round of pleasantries. Elanor was walking down the stairs from the office carrying a stack of boxes.

"Hey," I said. "Can I help you with that?"

"Sure," she said and handed me the entire stack. "On the counter." She turned and trudged back up the stairs.

I went through and put the boxes down. Mordecai followed me in.

"An irritating woman," he said with a sigh. "Though useful."

I nodded. "She's a lawyer, isn't she?"

81

"Yes. The best property lawyer in town." He ruffled the papers in his hand before laying them on the counter. "Have you made any further progress with your spell casting?"

My stomach knotted. Would he help me? I need to know more about what I'm actually doing, and he's the best source I have. "Yeah, actually. I'm not sure what it means, but…" I took a breath. "There's this eye enhancement spell they teach at school, night vision, distance seeing, that sort of thing."

Mordecai nodded. "I'm familiar with the type."

"Well, the other day when I twin-cast it, I did something to the spell form. I don't have a good way to describe it except that I inverted one of them."

His eyes narrowed, and his brow furrowed. "That did something?"

"No. Well, I don't know, because I realized that new form seemed to… fit with the standard spell form. So I merged them together."

He blinked. "The construct held? What did it do?"

"It was amazing. I could see everything like the standard spell, but there were all these colors, all over the place. It was like I could see auras, even magic itself!"

Mordecai's eyes bulged and his jaw dropped open. "True Sight?" he whispered. Then his features blanked. "Where did this happen?"

"At the drive-in, on Friday."

He nodded. The stairs creaked as Elanor descended once more.

"There was something else, I saw something that didn't look right. It drained the colors out of everything. I think it was a ghost."

"Did anyone else see this, ghost?"

"No, just me."

"Well then," he said. "No doubt it was some figment of your

imagination. Considering the colors you saw, it was likely a hallucination of sorts. Meddling with spell forms should not be done lightly, and you have zero experience with that sort of thing."

He reached into his pocket and pulled out a key ring as Elanor came out with another load of boxes. Mordecai separated a key and proffered it to her. "Here," he said. "This is a spare to the side door. I have a delivery of Azteca snuff coming tomorrow morning. Can you please deliver it to Ms Anderson as soon as it arrives?"

"Of course," she said as she took the key. "The entire shipment?"

"Yes. It's the easiest way to quiet her. There's another problem that's been giving me a lot of headaches, and I need to go out of town for a few days to wrap it up. After you make the delivery tomorrow, I won't need you until Wednesday morning. Now off with the both of you. I have a lot of paperwork to sort out."

Elanor collected her bag, and we left. "Shall we hit the library?" she asked. "It's still open for a few more hours. Maybe we can find out what happened to the St. John twins."

The list of things I wanted to do with Elanor that didn't involve the library swam through my mind. Then I heard Emily Ferguson's voice, asking me to find her sister. I took Elanor's hand and squeezed it. "Sure, sounds fun."

Chapter 13

WE SAT IN THE LAST BOOTH in the microfilm room, going through newspaper articles from a decade ago. The print-outs of what might be useful information lay on the table behind us. The library hadn't been busy when we came in. Now, about to close, it was empty.

Elanor stretched and looked up from the microfilm reader's screen. "I don't think there's anything more in that reel."

I pushed a few of the papers on the table around. "So this was a waste of time. Sandra St. John was a PhD student who published one paper on Fae cultural artifacts. Then she drops out of academic life, the phone book and everywhere else after one mention by a newspaper that the Ferguson deaths might be connected to the death and disappearance of her own daughters."

"True," she said. "But we found another suspicious twin death."

I picked up the print-out. "Fifty years ago Henry Reid and his twin brother, Morgan, disappeared. After a week of searching, Morgan's body was found in a collapsed river-bank cave. Henry was presumed dead, but apparently survived because sixty-two-year-old Henry was found dead, of natural causes, within a half-mile of where his brother died."

"Twins, one murdered, the other abducted." She sat at the

table next to me. "But not killed. He stayed alive for another fifty-three years until he returned home to die."

"And in all that time he never contacted his family, which is quite large apparently."

"There are a lot of Reids in that neck of the woods," she said as she jotted notes on a piece of paper. "So Morgan Reid died in a cave-in. If we follow the Fae elemental relationship idea, that would make him Earth."

"Henry had been dead for a few days when the hikers found him, and it took a month for dental records to identify him, which is why the cops never made a link even though he died on or about the same day that someone attacked the St. John twins."

"Right. Makasia St. John drowned in a river. That makes her Water. Her twin sister Violet was never found, just like Sarah Ferguson."

My mouth twisted up as an uncomfortable thought crossed my mind. "Do you think Violet and Sarah might still be alive somewhere?"

"Emily seemed pretty sure her sister was still alive," said Elanor. "I wish I knew how she was sure, though."

"Do you think they're linked somehow? The living to the dead?"

"Why would anyone do that?"

"Emily's ward. It needed some sort of power source, right? Why not use Sarah?"

Elanor blinked and bit her lip. "Perhaps," she said. "If these are all connected, then it has to be Fae work. There's a lot they can do that we don't understand."

"Was there anything about a long-lost twin being found around the time of the Ferguson's murder?"

"No, but if hikers hadn't come across Henry's body when they did, it might never have been recovered. So no news is not necessarily good news."

I nodded and leaned back in my chair to stretch out my sore back. "Speaking of news, Bethany showed up drunk to the memorial today."

"She must be going through hell," said Elanor.

"She looked awful, like she hadn't slept for a week." I cleared my throat. "Coach's speech wasn't bad," I said. "I wish you could've been there."

She shook her head. "No. I needed my space and a chance to focus on something else." She grimaced. "Although I didn't really want to spend half my day cleaning out Mordecai's stock room, that place is filthy."

"Did you see Bethany's mom when she came to the shop? She's in serious denial about her daughter's grief."

Elanor nodded. "My mom met her through the PTA when I re-joined the high school. She's amazing at her job and has ridiculously high standards."

"That explains why Bethany hates you," I said. "She was queen bee before you came back to school. She had to be to impress her own mother. When you showed up and your skill with magic blew everyone away…"

"Huh. Yes, that was about when she started flipping out, though she got super weird around Christmas." She frowned. "Bethany hates me? Like, actually hates me?"

"So she said. She set the whole thing up at the swim team party. She tricked me, convinced Jacob to ditch you, and unwittingly locked us both in with Emily."

Elanor frowned. "Bethany's mom is getting a delivery of Pixie Dust tomorrow to make up for her other shipments. What if her shipments weren't short? What if Bethany's been stealing it?"

"Pixie Dust? What's that? Some Fae medicinal thing?"

"Yes. Azteca tobacco contains a magical stimulant. It helps you focus and draw more magic than normal. It also gets you a bit high."

I laughed. "I'm surprised it's not illegal."

"It's like smoking a cigarette with magical nicotine. 'Pixie Dust' is when they grind it into a type of snuff instead of rolling it. You're supposed to be twenty-one to buy it." She frowned. "Apart from the lung damage, the only nasty side effect is a sense of paranoia and poor impulse control."

"If Bethany's been looking for an edge over you since the start of the school year, and her mom's been short on her recreational drugs…"

Elanor nodded. "That would explain a lot of her behavior."

"What if Bethany killed Jacob?"

"What?"

"Like at the park. You gave her a little smack talk, and she wanted to jump you. She got dumped by Jacob in front of us and almost attacked him with magic. Maybe she couldn't handle letting him go? She said he's been visiting her in her dreams. What if she killed him and linked his ghost to her, so they could be together forever?"

"That is bat-shit crazy."

"I know," I said. "But what about anything we're learning isn't?"

The librarian stuck her head in the room. "I'm getting ready to lock up. Oh, hello Elanor! Welcome back!"

"Thanks Ms. Castle," said Elanor. "How's everything going?"

"Oh, one mustn't complain, I suppose." She stepped into the room, a sheaf of loose printouts in her hand. "You were the young man who was researching the Ferguson fire for a class project, right?"

I nodded. "Yes, mam."

"I didn't realize you were working with Elanor. There was another young woman, came in yesterday. She asked for help to find a lot of the same information you did. I thought she was your partner."

"Did she give a name?"

"No. Blonde. A bit tall, spoke with an accent. And the amount of perfume she was wearing, my word! Elanor here is a delightful young lady who has already figured out that there is such a thing as too much scent, am I right?"

Elanor smiled. "The girls' restrooms can be a haze of spritz. I sometimes walk out smelling like a wildflower garden and all I did was wash my hands."

Ms. Castle nodded, her chins flapping. "I love the smell of lemons as much as anyone else, probably more, but there is a limit!" She shoved the sheaf of papers at me. "I found these fallen behind one of the work-desks. It looks to be about the fire. Is there anything you could use?"

"I don't know, but I'll look. Thank you."

She smiled at me. "Pleasant manners, for a boy, eh Elanor?" She winked, then lumbered out of the room. "Two minutes now. Else you'll be here until the morning!"

Elanor grabbed our printouts on the table. "That sounded a lot like Victoria, didn't it?"

I nodded. "She seems to be everywhere. At this point it would be a weird coincidence if it wasn't her." I quickly shuffled through the papers. "Most of these look familiar, I'll take them home and check them over with the stuff I already have."

"Alright," said Elanor. "I'll take this pile and see if I can tease out anything more about our disappeared Sandra St. John."

I frowned. "What's this?" Several of Victoria's printouts were of a family that was not the Ferguson's. In one, two dark-haired girls in pigtails were laughing and playing with a golden retriever. In another, they were with their mother in front of a big white house with a 'sold' sign.

"Looks like someone's social media stuff."

"Yeah, but twin girls? After what we've seen?"

Elanor stared at the picture. The hairs on my neck prickled

and my pants pocket felt warm. I pulled out the caged touch-stone. The crystals on the cage were shining.

"Oh shit!"

Elanor's eyes widened. "Quick, your True Sight spell!"

I dove up the magic and slipped on the True Sight goggles. The ghost stood in the doorway, balefire eyes staring at me. I lit a globe, reaching deep and pulling up a fire-hose of magic. My globe flared like an arc-welder. The ghost's eyes narrowed before it evaporated into oily strands of smoke.

Elanor was gripping my arm. "Cas. Where. Is. It?"

"It's gone," I said, and dropped the globe. "We're okay." I hugged her.

"Time to go, children," called Ms. Castle.

Chapter 14

THE STUTTERING ROAR of the gasoline engine drowned out the world. With my body distracted by pushing the mower through the overgrown yard, my brain could wander and think.

The ghost's appearance had scared the crap out of both of us, but after an hour of driving around, Elanor finally dropped me home. I was restless about her being alone. Even David asked if I was alright. Time crawled by until she sent to me that she was safe. I woke up every half-hour, but the new day dawned bright and clear, and with a phone call from the Johnson's asking if I could come over.

My neck tickled, and I felt Elanor Sending to me.

"Hey you," she said. Her smile glowed in my mind, warming my entire body.

"Morning." I let go of the mower brake and the motor sputtered to a stop. "You sleep okay?"

"Eventually. I made good use of the time, though. I got a lead on Sandra St. John."

"Awesome! How did you do that?"

"I pestered my dad. I told him I had found an article from a Fae scholar that was oh-so-interesting, but I couldn't find any more and since he's kinda in the field…"

I laughed. "And he came through. So what happened, Ms. St. John got married?"

"No. Mrs. St John got a divorce. Ms. Sandra Brown is the person whom we seek. Well, sought, because she's the curator of pre-colonial history at the Mint museum in Charlotte."

"Elanor, I…" My stomach flip-flopped.

"What is it?"

"That ghost scared the crap out of me last night. I don't want to walk away, but if there is a Fae killer on the loose, using that ghost, they know about us now."

Elanor was silent for a moment. "Whatever you decide," she said.

The thought of putting Elanor in danger scared the crap out of me. But they know about us already. Would they leave us alone if we back off? "The thought of having a summer, with you, and not worrying about anything else, that would be the best thing in the world."

"But," she said.

"But I have to follow this through. I can see the ghost, and they know it. That means that, eventually, they'll come after me. But you—"

"Will be right there with you."

I let out a deep breath I didn't remember taking. I let my relief and appreciation flow through the Sending, and felt a warm, comforting glow.

"I think it's great that you reached out to your dad," I said after a moment.

"Yes, well, just because he doesn't want to be involved in 'local matters' doesn't mean that us locals might not need him from time to time."

I could feel Elanor's happiness at having solved the riddle of the disappearing Sandra and at reconnecting with her father. I hoped we could spend some time together and this lawn might help. "Road trip? I can spring for gas money."

"Already ahead of you," she said. "I'm at the shop right now, waiting for the delivery guy. I'll swing by and pick you up. Then we can drop the Pixie Dust to Bethany's mom and head south." She made a face. "That gives you time to shower. I swear I need one myself after feeling how sweaty you are through this link."

"Sorry," I said. "I think you need to Send to me more often so I can practice not distracting you with my sweaty body while I do yard work, shirtless." I mentally flexed, like I was in front of a mirror.

She laughed. "Well, maybe I can be a bit distracted."

"Well, then you better come and watch in person. I've got to finish this lawn to get the gas money and I can't mow and chat at the same time."

"True. I don't want you to cut your own feet off. Then you'd be shorter than me. I'll see you soon." She blew a kiss and the connection ended.

I closed my eyes, took a deep breath, and smiled. The Sending had finished, but I felt connected to her still. Like a part of my heart had made room for her. A fresh wave of sweat broke out over my body. What if I was wrong about her, about us?

A half-hour later and I finished putting on some clothes after my quick but thorough shower. I scooped up the caged touch-stone and shoved it in my pocket. My wallet was a bit heavier with the Johnson's cash and my girl was on her way. I stopped at the bedroom door. My girl. The spot in my heart fluttered. "I hope," I whispered.

"Cas!" called Amy. "Elanor's here."

I hurried to the front door where Amy stood, waving to Elanor. "Have fun and be safe," she said to me.

David came from their bedroom. "Here," he said, handing me a folded twenty-dollar bill.

"I'm okay," I said. "The Johnson's paid up."

"It's for later," he said, pressing it into my hand. "In case you need it. We're going out tonight and might not be back until late."

"Thanks," I said. I squeezed the bill between my fingers. It was folded around something round, squishy and plastic covered. Oh. Oh! "Yeah, thanks." I slipped it into my wallet. "If I need to use it, I will. Promise."

He locked eyes with me. "You better."

Elanor chattered happily on the drive to Bethany's house. David's gift safely in my wallet but still burning a hole in my thigh. My mind was blank but my heart raced, my robot body smiling, nodding and staring at the world while the man behind the curtain ran around in circles screaming, in joy or fear I didn't know. The car was full of lilacs and her smile. When we stopped, she squeezed my knee.

"Hey, you okay?"

"Yeah, sorry." I got out of the car and grabbed the package from the rear seat. "I was thinking…"

"About what?"

About kissing you and more. "How are we going to play this? With Bethany's mom?"

Bethany's house was a two-story affair, overlooking the sixth hole of a golf course. Elanor pressed the doorbell, then pulled out a notebook and a pen from her back pocket. "Just follow my lead," she said.

"Yes mam."

Bethany's mom opened the door. "Hello Elanor, Cassius."

"Good morning Ms. Anderson," said Elanor. "We've got that shipment of Dust for you."

I hefted the box and smiled.

"Mordecai asked me to confirm the dates of the shipments that were short," said Elanor.

"Oh. Well do come in, and call me Abigail."

We walked into an entry hall that reminded me of the Ferguson's, complete with a grand staircase, but clad in bright white paint instead of ash.

"You can put it in there please, Cassius." She waved me to the library as she turned to Elanor. "Now, let's see. The first one was not long after Halloween…"

I put the box down on the coffee table next to a plush chaise-lounge. The bookshelves were fully loaded with a variety of books, many of them bound with well-worn leather. One set of shelves was dedicated to legal material, the other….

Abigail walked into the library and smiled. "A lot of those are first edition," she said.

"You have a wall of books about the Fae," I said. I glanced at Elanor, who had followed us into the library. "You must know a lot about them."

"They've always fascinated me. Their culture, their history," she said.

"Their magic," I said.

"Well, of course." Abigail picked out a hefty tome that smelled of old leather and showed me the cover. "Robinson's account of his journey through the Fae lands. Third edition, unfortunately, but in excellent condition for being three hundred years old. The insights are astounding."

"How's Bethany doing?" asked Elanor. "I've been thinking about her."

"Oh, she's fine. She's out right now, probably with her friends at the mall."

"She didn't seem so good when I saw her yesterday," I said. "At Jacob's memorial, she was in a bad way."

"Nonsense. Yes, of course she's not back to normal. Who could be in such a short time? But she's doing fine."

"I don't think she is Abigail," said Elanor. "I've only known Bethany for the last year, but even her girlfriends say she's been spiraling out for a while now."

"Well, I'm sure that's just school girl jealousy."

"Bethany showed up to the memorial drunk," I said. "Drunk,

and high. Everyone could see it."

Abigail stared at the leather-bound book in her hand.

"She admitted to me that she fell into a rivalry with Elanor over school work."

Elanor touched Abigail's shoulder. "Around Christmas, she got into a huge argument with another girl who used to be her best friend. She threatened her. With magic."

Abigail hugged the book to her chest.

"It all seems connected to when your shipments of Pixie Dust ran short."

A tear rolled down Abigail's face. "Because," she said. "If you use a lot in a short time, you get edgy, paranoid, and lose control." She shook her head. "I'm not blind. Not completely. I love my daughter and yes, there's been a problem and she won't talk to me about it." She slumped onto the chaise-lounge. "I've felt so helpless."

"I know this stuff boosts you up," I said. "But with it also making her more angry, explosive, well…"

"Well, what?"

"Getting dumped by Jacob hurt her, do you think that it's—"

"Don't you dare finish that sentence," she snapped, face flushing red. She stood up. "I will talk to my daughter about what's going on, but if you even think that way again I will throw your ass in juvie, don't think I can't find a way."

"I'm so sorry," I said as we backed away to the front door.

"If you're looking for a scapegoat, look at that swim team kid, Reed Williams. From what I hear, he was the one who called the cops. Jacob must have gotten word from the bookie's spotters and panicked."

"We're so sorry to have upset you," said Elanor.

"Just go." The door slammed shut. The sound of crying came faintly through.

Chapter 15

WE DROVE IN SILENCE UNTIL Elanor merged us onto I-85 and we were solidly on the way to Charlotte. We found some rocking tunes on the radio, cranked it, and yelled and sang our way out of the funk.

"Okay, okay," said Elanor as she turned the volume down. "Remind me not to have you on my team at karaoke night!"

I laughed, my voice a bit raw. "Yeah? Well, that high-c you were trying for fell a little flat on that last one." I squeezed her knee, and she smiled.

"You're too kind," she said and grinned. "Because that was an absolute mess."

"Okay, so no karaoke dates then."

"I think that would be best."

*****

The miles rolled away and we arrived at the Mint. Walking through the glassed entryway, we stopped at the reception desk to pay our entry fee.

"Is Dr Brown in today?" asked Elanor. "I read one of her articles on Fae culture and I was hoping to speak to her if she was available."

"Yes, she is," said the receptionist. "She's on lunch, but she'll be back in a few minutes. You can wait in the library. She has to go through there to get to her office."

"Thank you," I said.

We headed to the library, but stopped at an exhibit of Fae clothing through the ages. Replicas of simple but well-made clothing became increasingly complex, floral, colorful, then shockingly monochromatic, plain, severe, before softening again and becoming incredibly baroque, even fractal.

"Absolutely stunning, aren't they?" said a woman. "From the Undying Dynasty period. These are replicas, but made in the Fae lands using original patterns."

"They're beautiful," said Elanor.

I pointed at a complex set of knotwork. "It looks like there are crystal beads woven in, is that Babingtonite?"

"Yes! Well spotted," said the woman. "They're layered throughout the fabric. When energized they form the sigils of various houses and the individual bloodlines within them."

"It must have been an amazing sight to see an entire room of these lit up," said Elanor. "But then it all goes more plain until it's the same as what we wear."

"True, but after nearly two thousand years of wearing the same clothes, do you blame them for wanting a change?"

My eyes widened. "Two thousand years?"

She nodded. "The Undying Court was the height of their culture and world-wide civilization. We humans were still in the stone-age. It all fell apart, of course."

"Why?"

"The Fae had extended their lifespans through magic. Unfortunately, this bounty meant that their culture and society solidified. They didn't just resist change, they ignored it completely." She shook her head. "You can only ignore change for so long. According to the legends they've shared, a great evil arose. A betrayer. A usurper. A would-be tyrant who raised an army of demons and shattered the heart of the Undying Court."

"And this new tyrant put an end to the life-extension magic?"

"No. They practice it still, but nowhere near the extent they used to. They came to understand the damage to their society that near immortality brought. Most now only live for two to three centuries, and they retreat from society past a certain age to ensure the young can take their place." She smiled. "Is that what you wanted to talk to me about?"

"Dr. Sandra Brown?"

"That's me."

Elanor and I looked at each other. Elanor cleared her throat. "You used to be a St. John though, right?"

The smile faded. "Yes." She frowned. "Cindy said you had read a paper of mine and had questions. The only paper I ever published under that name was my post-doc, and that wasn't exactly ground-breaking stuff."

"It's not about your paper, per se," said Elanor. "It's about the Fae that took your daughter, Makasia."

Sandra's face froze. "You two need to leave," she hissed. "Now."

"Please," Elanor said. "There is something going on and—"

Sandra turned on her heel and stalked towards the entrance. "I'm calling security."

"We've seen the giant of smoke and fire," I said.

Sandra stopped at the doorway.

"It looks like a human, or a Fae. Ten feet tall. Living, writhing, oily smoke with two eyes of fire. And it's pure evil."

Sandra turned back, her face blank. "I never told anyone about that."

I pulled out the caged touch-stone. "It killed a friend of ours. I got a sample of its aura but..."

Sandra reached out and took the touch stone. She released it from its cage for a moment, then slammed it back in. Tears welled in her eyes and streamed down her face. "Oh my god. Oh my god, that was real." She wiped at her face. "Come. Come to my office and we'll talk. Oh my god."

Chapter 16

SANDRA SAT IN HER OFFICE CHAIR, eyes fixated on the caged touch-stone on her desk as Elanor and I told her of our meeting with the ghost of Emily Ferguson, and Jacob's murder.

"And so with everything pointing towards some type of Fae magic, you found me because of one comment in a newspaper article."

"Yeah," I said. "I know it sounds far-fetched—"

"That one stupid little comment."

Elanor and I looked at each other.

"That one comment cost me my marriage." She looked up at last. "The horror, the nightmare of it all, of losing them both was bad enough. But Henry, when the press started focusing on what I had said and making it out like it was an excuse, he couldn't handle it anymore. It broke him. That somehow I might have been negligent, been responsible for their deaths." Her body shook as tears rolled down her face.

"Why did you say it?" asked Elanor.

"When I was pregnant, I realized I had a talent." Sandra wiped her face. "I had a powerful connection with my girls. I could always feel them, always know where they were. I know lots of mothers have something similar, at least for a while, but most fade. My connection grew stronger. When they got their magic, I could even see their auras."

"That's a rare gift," said Elanor.

"Yes, and it's how I knew there was a problem. One minute they were in the car with the nanny, the next, nothing. I tried to reach out and find them, but it was like they never existed. Then Makasia came to me, flew up to me screaming and crying right through the wall of my bedroom." Sandra's eyes fixated on a memory. "Then that, that thing showed up." She shoved the touch-stone away from her and buried her face in her hands.

I reached out and pocketed the touch-stone.

"Please," said Elanor. "What happened next?"

Sandra let out a breath. "It grabbed Makasia. There was a blue leash or something it connected to her. Everything jerked away in a flash and, well, that was that. She was gone. It happened so fast I didn't even know if I'd seen it or imagined it."

"What happened to the nanny?" I asked. "Was she involved?"

"No," said Sandra, shaking her head. "She loved those girls. They found the car on a service road, next to the river. Helen was inside the car, dead. Brain aneurysm. They found tracks of the girls going down to the river, but nothing else."

"And this thing you saw. That's what made you think it was the Fae, right? Why?"

Sandra stood up and pulled out a well-worn book from a bookshelf with a familiar cover. "Robinson's Journal," she said as she flipped through it, then placed it open on the desk. Fae script filled one page. A drawing of a giant made of smoke and fire dominated the other.

"No way," whispered Elanor.

"It's proper name is Ketepani, which roughly translates as 'Ancient Servant', but the more common term is Golem."

I stared at the picture. "That's the thing I saw. That's what killed Jacob."

Elanor was frowning at the Fae script. "So, it's a construct of some sort?"

"Yes," said Sandra. "A living spell form, tied to its master with a permanent connection. And because of that, it can continue to exist even when its owner is asleep."

"A permanent connection?" I asked. "So it's always pulling power from its owner?"

"Yes," she said. "So far as we know, only the Fae can make them. It's related to their life extension magic." She flipped through the book until she landed on a page showing a tall tree marked with a Fae rune. "There. By connecting themselves to something that lives far longer, they extend their own lives."

I frowned, but Elanor nodded. "Some species of trees live for hundreds, if not thousands of years."

"But it's not a connection of their magic, like with the Golem. It's their actual life force." Sandra sat down. "I like to think it's a good thing that we've never figured out how to meddle with that."

"Living for a thousand years might not be all bad," I said.

"On an individual level? Perhaps. Perhaps not. On a societal level? Disastrous." She stood up and returned the book to its place on the shelf. "Remember the clothing exhibit? Their rise and ultimate, catastrophic fall was because of a ruling class that refused to die off, and strictly stratified their entire society to support it. We still see echoes of that even today, such as the Gifting Ceremony."

I frowned. "That's some sort of ceremonial rent for part of North Carolina, but it's just a tourist thing, isn't it?"

"Not entirely," said Elanor. "Some of my dad's work documents refer to parts of the entire country as Fae territories."

Sandra nodded. "That's right. The Fae ruled the entirety of North America when the first human colonists landed here. They ceded certain lands to us, and we won others by proxy wars with the Fae-backed Native Americans. But the Fae simply abandoned a good chunk of America as they shifted their civilization north."

"They never renounced the land," said Elanor. "Which for a species that lives as long as the Fae is the same as you or I going on vacation, then coming back and finding squatters in your house."

"So we're actually paying them rent," I said.

Sandra nodded. "A token rent, but yes, and it wasn't always tobacco leaves. Originally it was people."

Elanor's eyes bulged. "What?!"

"Those old wives tales about stolen kids aren't without a kernel of truth. They weren't kidnappings, they were rent payments." She shook her head. "Hostages, really. Oh, we've had similar things in our own histories, so it shouldn't be that hard to swallow."

"Yeah," I said. "Feudal lords in England used to hold on to each other's kids to keep the neighbors from attacking them."

"That's right. The upper tiers of Fae society would have a bevy of lower-class servants bound to them. There were strict rules about the classes mixing. They had an absolute phobia about being exposed to auras from the lower classes for fear of being tainted."

"They thought their auras would be affected?" Elanor frowned. "That doesn't seem right."

Sandra shrugged. "Their concern was that if there were enough lowborn in one place, the concentration would override one's natural defenses. There were many stories about highborn Fae acting strange because of too much exposure, or even being possessed by a cabal of the lower class."

My chest tightened. A strong magical aura influencing a weaker one? I looked at Elanor and my stomach clenched. Could I have done that? Could I be doing that right now?

"Sandra," said Elanor. "Something we were hoping you could help us with was a ceremonial calendar. Each of the deaths we know about seems to connect with an element. The Fergusons by fire, your daughter by water, and we even found reference to another set of twins, Henry and Morgan Reid, who would be earth."

"I see where you're going with this. Yes, there is such a book which might help, but we don't have a copy. It's called the Pitokwe, or 'Shadow Memory'. It's a collection of insights from those who lived among the Fae as their hostages. There are only a few authentic copies out there. I heard through the grapevine one went up for private auction recently, but I have no idea who has it."

Elanor and I looked at each other. "We need some time to think all this through," she said. "Can we contact you later if we have more questions?"

"Of course," said Sandra.

As we stood to leave, I pointed at Robinson's Journal. "That doesn't have actual instructions on how to do Fae magic, does it?"

"No," said Sandra. "It's more of a Marco Polo style travelogue. Lots of cultural knowledge, but nothing practical." We all shook hands. "I don't know how much I've helped you, but if there's anything else I can do, please let me know."

"If we find anything that might help explain what you saw," I said. "I promise we'll let you know."

"You need to promise me to be very, very careful. A Golem is a dangerous thing, but it only does as it's told. If its master knows that you know about it…" her voice trailed off.

My throat tightened as I tried to keep a straight face. "I don't think anyone knows that we know anything." I paused. "And we know nothing at all, really."

"And there's no point in talking to the police," said Elanor. "We have no actual proof of anything."

Sandra nodded. "If I thought otherwise, I'd already have sent to them."

She walked us out of the building, and we returned to the car. We sat there for a few minutes in silence, trying to put things together. Elanor stared at her hands on the steering wheel, bottom lip between her teeth, a strand of her red hair escaping her ponytail. I reached out and tucked it behind her ear. She twitched, then smiled and grabbed my hand and kissed it. "Sorry," she said.

The touch of her lips warmed my skin, and all I wanted to do was pull her close and kiss her, hard. I could see a spark in her eyes and felt our breathing fall in sync. Does she want to kiss me, or is it because I want her to? I looked away and took my hand back. "If we get going now, we can beat the dinner rush at the diner."

She sat there for a moment before starting the car. "Yes, we better start back. Don't want to miss dinner."

"I'm a growing boy," I said. "I'm always hungry."

She rolled her eyes and we pulled back onto the road.

Chapter 17

ELANOR WAS QUIET ON THE DRIVE BACK. I wasn't feeling much like talking either. I felt hollow inside at the thought that Elanor's feelings for me might not be entirely her own.

After an hour I finally reached to turn on the radio. Her eyes caught mine for a second, but she nodded. Music helped to fill the silence for a minute, then she turned the volume down. "Is everything okay?"

"What? Yeah, everything's fine." I frowned. "Are you okay?"

"I'm not the one with a problem," she said.

What the hell? I opened my mouth to say something; she shushed me and turned up the radio.

"Police have released the name of the young male found drowned in a neighbor's pool early this morning. Reed Williams, sixteen, was pronounced dead at the scene. Police are appealing for witnesses to this tragic accident. In other news—" I stabbed the radio's off button.

"Oh my god," Elanor said. Her face had gone pale.

"Reed's dead?" I shook my head. "Drowned? How? He was on the swim team!"

"Was he drinking? They might not have released that yet."

Unbidden, I imagined trying to swim, the water smashing into me, forcing me under, stealing my breath. Just like my last swim practice. "Bethany," I said.

"What?"

"At the last team practice. The day you came back from your trip? I was doing laps and the water got rough. Turns out it was Bethany messing with my lane. It was right in the middle of practice and nobody caught it because she was being subtle. If she'd tried to hurt me…." A chill ran down my neck.

"That's what she and Jacob argued about, right? Her messing with you when you and Jacob were racing."

"Yeah. Bethany slammed Reed hard at the memorial. But you heard her mom blame Reed for Jacob's death. If Bethany got that into her head—"

"She might have played nice to get him alone, then killed him." Elanor nodded. "If she's strung out on Pixie Dust, she's capable of anything."

We drove the next few miles in silence. As we approached Greensboro, my thoughts drifted back to before the radio station. I'd upset her, somehow. I could let it go, but should I?

"Hey," I said. A wailing cry filled my ears as a figure of smoke and fire careened down the highway towards us.

"Oh shit!" Elanor pumped the brakes, swerved to dodge. My head slammed into the door, then my body crushed into the car seat as she floored it.

The ghost's screaming intensified. I dove for the magic, but everything fuzzed. "Cas! Snap out of it!" Elanor was yelling, but she sounded far away. I swallowed and inhaled deeply. As I breathed out, the world refocused. "I'm here," I said, looking around. "Where is it?"

"I don't know, but I can feel it!"

My eyes widened. A trail of smoke trickled through the roof of the car above Elanor's head. The thought of Jacob, his life snuffed out at a touch, flashed before my eyes. A tsunami of anger and magic surged through me. The world shifted to a kaleidoscope of colors. The dead gray ghost flew above the car, reaching down to drain my Elanor's golden glow.

"Not today, bitch!" I screamed. The globe burst from my hand into a torrent of ethereal light that pierced the roof of the car and seared the ghost, flaying the smoke and fire from its core. It bellowed in pain, a familiar voice from a familiar face. *Jacob?*

Magic surged from the ghost. The fire and smoke reformed as it grabbed my neck. Fire burned my skin and smoke choked my lungs, drowning me. The scream of rage deafened me. The light of the magic flickered. Something grabbed my arm. Elanor! I grabbed back, channeled the magic through to her, felt her mesh. The ghost's rage forced me down into the depths of darkness, the pressure overwhelming. My connection to Elanor became distant, small, and started to drift away. *Elanor... help....*

A beam of golden light pierced the smoke, slicing the ghost away from me. My chest loosened, and I sucked in a lungful of air. The world snapped into focus, the ghost on my chest, stumps of smoke around my neck. Electricity crackled as I charged my hands with magic. I grabbed the ghost, reaching through the fire and smoke to its core. I could feel a pulsing connection like a starving leach, feeding the ghost. Feeding Jacob.

"Leave. Us. Alone!" I screamed. I pulsed the magic through my hands, trying to rip his aura apart. Jacob screamed, struggling to escape. One hand lashed out and smashed into my head. The world retreated, as if through a tunnel, and I felt Jacob slip away.

I sat boneless in my chair, drained and quivering. Elanor held my hand. The car wasn't moving. We were on the side of the highway, under a bridge. Other cars sped by, oblivious.

Elanor trembled, tears running down her face. We pulled each other close, my face buried in her hair. The smell of her calmed me, the touch of her skin warmed me. In her arms I knew I was safe, and for the first time in a long time, whole.

Chapter 18

ELANOR'S HOUSE WAS A RAMBLING one-story ranch that sat alone on a vast field of tightly trimmed grass. As we parked in the driveway, automated lights switched on in a futile attempt to drive off the coming night.

"You sure your mom isn't here?" I asked.

"Yes. She left for the spa without me."

We got out of the car and went inside. In the fridge was half a pizza, which we warmed and ate. Sitting at the table, I could finally process what I had seen into words.

"That was Jacob, right? I wasn't hallucinating. Was I?"

Elanor's face froze, then she sobbed. "I think it was," she said as fresh tears flowed. "But how?"

I held her hand. "There was a connection. I could feel it, fueling him."

Elanor wiped her face. "Bethany. She's using the Dust to boost her magic. She's letting Jacob feed on her."

"How can she be connected to him? She wasn't even there."

Elanor frowned. "When Jacob died, you said there was that bolt of magic. That could have been a connection forming with Bethany."

"This isn't making sense. If that was a golem that killed Jacob, Bethany's golem, she could have forged the connection at a distance, right? Then why kill Reed? It's not like she could blame him for Jacob's death."

Elanor shook her head. "I don't think Bethany's in any sort of rational state. Killing Jacob, that has to mess with her head in so many ways. I can't even comprehend what might be in that girl's mind right now." We headed for the lounge. "Her aura must be so twisted."

We sat on the couch, Elanor curling up against me with her head on my chest. "Could we ward the room, together?"

I put my arm around her shoulders. "Of course." I hesitated before dipping my toe in the magic.

"You okay?" she asked.

"I'm not sure what I did in the car," I said. "I don't want to push too hard."

"Oh! Yes, okay. Nevermind then, it's fine."

"No," I said. "I want you to be safe." I relaxed and let the magic flow through me. I held Elanor's hand. "Go on."

Our auras meshed. A crystal cage formed around the room, enclosing us, protecting us. Elanor relaxed against me as it sealed us away from the world. Elanor's touch on our magic was gentle and warm. I ran my fingers through her soft hair. We locked eyes, our breathing falling in sync. The thump of my heart pulsed in my ears. Pulling her close, I could feel her heartbeat match mine. Our lips touched, gently. Then again, firmly. Our arms tightened around each other and she straddled me, her breasts pressed against my chest. I responded, my skin flushing with heat. I wanted her. Oh god, how I wanted her. Oh god. I wanted. Does she want this? Or is this just me?

I broke off the kiss and took a deep, shuddering breath. "I think maybe we should slow down."

Her beautiful eyes were full of hurt and confusion. "I'm sorry," she said and rolled off me, scooting to the other end of the couch. "What did I do wrong? Or," a note of anger crept into her voice. "Or is there something wrong with me?"

I shook my head. "You did nothing wrong, and you're perfect—"

"Then what's going on?" she demanded. "You froze me out in the car at the Mint, and now this. Do you not want to be with me? Is there somebody else?"

"No! Of course not!"

"Then what is it?"

I opened my mouth. My head pounded. What could I say?

"Talk to me!"

"Sandra!"

"What?"

"No. Something she said. She told us about the Fae, about how worried they were about their aura's being influenced. About being controlled by another, doing things they didn't really want to do."

Elanor stared at me.

I reached out and she let me take her hand. "There is nobody else in the world for me," I said. "Only you. I want to be with you. I want that so badly."

"But," she said.

"But there's also no denying that my aura compared to yours, there's a big difference. Am I influencing you? Am I causing you to feel you want me, even if you don't?"

Her face lost all expression. "So you don't trust me to know myself."

"I don't trust me," I said. "All the foster parents I've lived with. I expected them to go rotten, and they did. Every single one. You expect a few bad apples in the system. There are only so many people willing to be a foster parent. But every single one? Since I was nine and got my magic? What are the odds?" I shook my head. "David and Amy were on the same track. I could name the date when my case worker would've showed up. Then I fell for you," I squeezed her hand. "I didn't want them to be rotten, because I would have had to move to another city and lose you." She squeezed my hand back and gave me the hint of a smile. "I needed David to fix things, and he found a way. They're back on track, out on a date night."

Elanor bit her lip and looked away from me. "Okay," she said. "Okay."

"I'm scared, alright? I don't want to lose you. I don't want to wake up tomorrow and you tell me it's over because we did something that, deep down, you didn't want to—"

"Okay, I get it," she said. She took a breath, held it, and let it go. "I get it. But it still hurts that you don't trust me to know myself." She turned on the TV and started flicking through channels.

I shut up and stared at the TV without watching. She was mad, and she had every right to be. But I wasn't a rapist, and that's what it would be without her being sure. Would there be any way to know, though? How sure can I—

"Wait, go back a sec," I said.

Elanor frowned, but back-tracked a channel. "You want to watch the news?"

A reporter stood outside a house, while police milled about. "No updates yet from police about the twin girls kidnapped tonight from a home in north Greensboro. We can confirm they were reported missing by their father, who came home from grocery shopping to find his wife dead, and his twin girls missing."

"That house," I said. "That's the house Victoria was looking at. It was in the stack of pictures she printed at the library."

"Oh my god," whispered Elanor. "You're right."

Ice ran down my spine. "More twins. How the hell is Victoria mixed up in this? You said she was running a glamour about her perfume. Could she be doing more? Could she be a Fae in disguise?"

Elanor's eyes were wide. "I don't know. Maybe? Normally you'd notice something like that because it would take tons of juice. But if she ran it inverted, like the wards were? We'd never know."

The Fae killer we were looking for had her next pair of victims.

"We've got to find her," I said. "Before she kills again."

"How? We've got no sample of her aura. We don't know where she's staying. If it is her and she's following a ritual, we don't know what element she's going to use. She could be anywhere!"

I jumped as the telephone jangled.

"That better not be my mother," said Elanor as she stalked to the kitchen. "I do not have time for her right now."

I stood up and paced. Could Victoria be the killer? She was direct, no question about that. She was from the Fae lands. I haven't seen her do magic, so I don't know how strong she is. Though from what Mordecai was trying to hook me on, the Fae are amazing at everything. Mordecai. He sponsored Victoria's trip here. Is he involved? I stared at the TV, hoping for inspiration, but all it showed me was a county commissioner complaining about his car being stolen from the airport parking lot.

"Cas!" called Elanor from the kitchen. "Come here!"

Chapter 19

I RUSHED INTO THE KITCHEN. Elanor was at the table with the phone. "Okay," she said. "You're on speaker, please say that again."

"I can't find her," sobbed Abigail through the phone. "She came home not long after you left. I confronted her about stealing the Dust. We had a fight, but she admitted to taking it. I tried to talk her down, but she was out of control and she bolted!" She took a long, quavering breath. "I tried to Send to her, but she blocked me. She blocked me all day, but at least that was something! She showed up an hour ago and started tearing the place apart. She was yelling about Jacob being hurt, about him dying. I tried to tell her," she hiccuped. "To say he was already dead and…"

"And what, Abigail?" asked Elanor.

"She attacked me! Punched me. And the screaming! She wanted more Dust, but I told her I didn't have any. That it was all gone." Her voice dropped to a whisper. "She used magic. Threw me across the room."

"Oh my god," I said. "That's crazy!"

"By the time I got my head straight, she was gone. She needs help, but if I call the police about this," she said, sobbing. "Oh my poor little girl, I don't know what to do!"

"What do you mean, she's gone?" said Elanor. "She's still blocking you?"

"No. I can feel that. It's like she's not even there. Like she's behind a ward, but she doesn't know how to do that. She's never been good at wards."

"Mrs Anderson," I said. "I don't know how to explain this, but I need to ask a question that might be important. You've got a lot of books about Fae lore. Do you have a copy of the Pitokwe?"

She laughed. "No, I wish. Mordecai got to it first. How is that important?"

"Mordecai, who owns Migina's?"

"Yes."

Thoughts were running through my head faster than I could catch them. I signaled to Elanor to end the call.

"I think I know one place to look for her," said Elanor. "I'm guessing though. You should stay home in case she comes back. We'll go see and, if she's there, we'll Send to you, I promise."

"Okay," said Abigail. "I think I need to call the cops. This is too much." She hung up.

"Where do you think Bethany is?"

"The only source of Dust in town is Mordecai's shop. And if Mordecai has a copy of the Pitokwe there, now would be a great time to use Bethany as an excuse to go snooping."

I smiled. "You're amazing," I said and held out my hand to her.

She took it. "I'm still mad at you, but we're okay."

"Promise?"

"Promise."

She grabbed her keys and we broke our link, dissolving the ward. As we left the house the humid night air was so thick I almost choked.

"Okay," I said as we pulled out onto the main road. "So Bethany attacking her mom with magic proves that she's flipped out enough to have killed Jacob and Reed."

"Yes," said Elanor. "But she doesn't have the Pitokwe. No book., no Fae magic, no Golem to order around. And there's no way she could've bound Jacob's ghost to herself. From what I've figured out that kind of connection is like what I did when I trapped Emily's ghost. It's a type of warding magic—"

"Which she's crap at," I said. "She looked awful at the memorial. The link was killing her. It…"

"What? What is it?"

"The memorial. Victoria was there, and she left with Reed."

We were approaching downtown. Elanor said nothing for a moment as she pulled off the main road and parked. "Victoria killed Reed? Why?"

"I don't know. It doesn't make any sense. Maybe she didn't, maybe that was Bethany. Could she have drained his life force to keep Jacob alive?"

We got out of the car. "This way," said Elanor. "The alley leads to the shop's side entrance."

The light from the main road slashed into the darkness of the alleyway. We passed by a dumpster that reeked of rancid meat, then came to the alley beside Migina's. A bright pink VW Bug was parked next to the open side entrance.

"That her car?" I asked.

"Yes. She rubbed it in our faces months ago when she got her license."

I stepped through the side entrance into the staff kitchen and fumbled for the light switch. It clicked, but the lights didn't turn on. I popped a globe and stepped forward; something crunched underfoot. Glass. Looking up, I saw the overhead lights had burst.

"Looks like someone blew a fuse," I whispered.

Elanor rolled her eyes.

We walked into the store's showroom. The place was a mess; shattered overhead lights and shelf contents knocked onto the floor. The medicine dispensary where Mordecai kept his imported herbs and remedies had one door torn off, revealing a hidden mini-fridge. Ripped plastic packets mixed with shattered glass and unidentifiable powders. The room was silent. Nothing moved.

"Where now?" I whispered as we returned to the passageway.

Elanor pointed down the steps. Basement. Right. She grabbed my hand and leaned on me while she looked at the bottom of her shoe.

"What are you doing?"

"I must have stepped in something. I swear I can still smell that rancid pork from the alleyway. It's making me sick."

I squeezed her hand as we descended into the darkness. At the bottom, the smell of rotting meat filled the air. A shadow moved against the far wall.

I raised my globe. "Bethany?"

Elanor gasped. "Oh my god!"

On the floor lay a corpse, dressed in fashionable clothes. Her blonde hair streamed out of the floor, pulled away from the skull. The blackened skin bubbled and liquefied as we stared. Over it hovered a miasma of oily smoke. The smoke cloud opened eyes of fire, and the ghost of Jacob shrieked.

Chapter 20

THE MAGIC WELLED UP WITHIN ME, but the ghost was faster. A tentacle of oily smoke lashed out. I dove right. Elanor's scream turned into a gurgle.

The ghost had her by the neck, pulsating tendrils of smoke and fire piercing the barrier she kept trying to build. I formed a knife as I scrambled to my feet and hurled it at the tentacle. It severed the connection for a moment but it reformed.

Elanor dropped to her knees, her head lolling back, shoulders falling limp.

"Nooo!"

I popped a globe, filling it with my rage and magic until it exploded. The miasma shrouding the ghost blew away like smoke in a hurricane, evaporating the tentacles. Elanor fell to the floor like a discarded rag doll.

I knelt down and grabbed her arm. "Elanor! Wake up!" Pain lashed my back with a red-hot baseball bat and I fell on top of her, gasping for air.

The ghost hovered over Bethany's decaying corpse. It was Jacob. A bloated, twisted, horrific version, but him. His arm elongated as he swung a fist of knobbed flesh and claws. I popped a globe to block, but it smashed right through, shattering the construct and what felt like every bone in my right hand.

Jacob screamed in triumph, then swung again. I raised my left arm to block, shaping my magic into a shield. The blow against the shield rang through me like a church bell, but it held. I extended the shield to cover Elanor. Blow after blow rained down like anvils, but the shield did not break.

"Elanor! Please, you've got to wake up!"

The attacks ceased. Jacob screamed at me. Bethany's body was down to skin pierced by cracked bones. I popped the True Sight spell. Elanor was a pale, pale gold, but there was a glimmer inside. She lived. She just needed help.

I looked at Jacob. His twisted aura was fragmenting, but a tendril leashing him to Bethany's corpse delivered a trickle of red. Of course! He had survived this long by draining her life force. Now he was sucking the energy from the very marrow of her bones. When that finished, so was he. I could wait him out, but Elanor couldn't.

I stood up. The nerves in my right hand were on fire, but my fingers could move.

"I'm sorry, Jacob. But you gotta go."

I focused on Bethany's corpse. "I hope there's enough left to bury you." I formed elemental fire beads on my thumb and index fingertips. Bone grated on bone as I pressed them together. I grit my teeth against the pain, snapped my fingers, and set Bethany's corpse ablaze.

Jacob's shrieked and flailed as the roaring flames burnt out the last traces of Bethany's life-force. Starved of energy, Jacob wailed and dissolved into the vestiges of ash and billowing soot.

Elanor was still out of it, the glimmer sputtering. I knelt down, pinched her nose shut and breathed into her mouth. Her chest rose. I let the air out and did it again. And again. The glimmer stopped flickering, but she was barely breathing on her own.

"Come on, think!" There has to be something I can do. I cradled my right hand, pulses of pain throbbing their way up my arm. Tears rolled down my face, the salt bitter on my tongue. Bitter. Coach.

I stumbled to my feet and ran up the stairs to the dispensary. Powders and dried herbs lay scattered, but I needed a liquid. I opened the mini-fridge. There! The jar's label was in Fae script, but underneath were the words "Queen of Bitter". I unscrewed the top and took a small sip. The smell was minty, but the blue liquid was brine. I choked it down. Almost immediately, my hand hurt less.

Dashing back down the stairs I knelt by Elanor, her glow almost faded, and poured a trickle into her mouth. "Come on, come on."

Nothing. Then she jerked. I helped her to roll on her side as she coughed and wheezed. Her eyes finally opened. I helped her to sit up against me and got her to drink some more.

She coughed. "I take it you won?" she whispered.

"Yeah. We won."

"I don't think getting hit by a bus counts as helping to win."

I smiled. "I'll take whatever help I can get. I can't do this without you." Tears trickled down my face at the thought of Elanor lying there, cold and lifeless. "I can't. Not without you."

She nestled against me. "That stuff tastes awful."

"I know. Coach told me about it. I'm thankful Mordecai had it in stock."

Elanor sat up. I offered the jar to her, but she shook her head. "I'm fine. I don't think you're supposed to have as much as I did at one go. I can feel myself getting wired like I'm going to have to go for a run." She shivered, and even without the True Sight I could feel her aura shine. "You have some more."

I choked down the last mouthful and felt warmth spread throughout my body, drowning the pains and burns. We held onto each other as we stood up.

"Poor Bethany," said Elanor.

"Yeah," I said. "Look, I'm not sure how to handle this. We told her mom we'd Send to her but…"

"I know," Elanor said. "That would involve the cops. Trying to tell them what happened would lose us hours, and the life of one of those twins."

"Okay, so it's just us."

"Yes. So we better go find that book."

Chapter 21

THE ONLY PLACE LEFT TO SEARCH was upstairs, in Mordecai's office. The stairs creaked as we ascended. A flick of the switch and we had lights.

"I guess she never made it up here," I said.

The second floor somewhat mirrored the first. Stairwell, toilet, kitchenette, but there were two doors off the passageway.

Elanor pointed. "Left is storage. That's where I was pulling boxes to stock the shelves the other day. It's pretty empty. Right is his office suite."

I reached my hand out to open the office door, then stopped.

"What's wrong?"

"I don't need any more surprises tonight," I said and popped the True Sight goggles. The door continued to look like a door, so I opened it.

The reception area featured an old leather sofa, with a pillow and blanket wadded up on it, a bank of filing cabinets and a closed door to Mordecai's inner office. "Looks clear," I said and entered.

"Let's check the filing cabinets first," said Elanor. The drawers were unlocked. It didn't take us long to flick through them all.

"Lots of records about lots of things," I said. "But no book."

"Talk about an old family business," said Elanor. "Some of these records go back nearly a hundred and fifty years."

We opened the door to the last room. Mordecai's actual office was sparse: a table used as a desk, and a chair. A small side-table by a window held a bonsai tree and a water spritzer. The bonsai tree glowed with an inner light.

"Okay, that's weird," I said.

"What is it?"

"That bonsai has a powerful aura. Like a person's aura."

Elanor studied the tree. "It looks normal to me," she said. "There's a Fae rune on the pot. I don't know it but it looks familiar."

"It looks like the rune on the tree in Robinson's journal...." I blinked as realization struck. "Oh crap. Mordecai is in on this."

Elanor frowned. "How?"

"The tree has a person's aura. Mordecai's aura. As long as it lives, he lives."

She nodded. "Juniper Bonsai's can live for centuries. He sponsored Victoria's visit, so she could come here, kidnap a set of twins and murder one of them."

"She's going to disappear tonight, with the surviving twin, back to the Fae lands."

"We need that book. Now," said Elanor.

"It's not here," I said. "But maybe we don't. When I was last here, I overheard Bethany's mom. She had closed a property deal for Mordecai and was handing over the paperwork."

Elanor nodded. She returned to the file cabinets, browsing. "Here," she said after a moment, pulling open one of them. She flicked through the contents, pulled out a file and brought it back to the table. She pulled out the first set of paperwork. "Got it. Here's the address."

My eyes fixated on the next page in the open folder. "And there's a proof he's involved." It was a completed contract of sale for the Ferguson's McMansion, dated two months after the fire that covered up the ritual murder of Emily Ferguson.

My knees buckled. "Oh my god, this is all our fault." I tried to swallow the lump in my throat and choked. "It's all my fault!"

Elanor was there, holding me. "We, you, are not responsible for what happened."

"We were there. Bethany and Jacob used magic to force me in and blocked the door. We got trapped by the ward because I was stupid and tried to blow my way out." Tears rolled down my cheeks. "When we got Emily out, the ward broke and wiped itself out. You said it. There wasn't a trace of anything inside the house. Inside!"

"There wasn't." Elanor took a sharp breath. "Which means there was no trace of us being in the house. Just the residue of Jacob and Bethany's magic outside."

"Mordecai must have been alerted when the ward flatlined. He got there in time to take a sample of their auras, like I did with the golem."

"Then he called in Victoria to come clean up the mess and help him with another set of twins," said Elanor. "This is insane!"

"Does any of this make sense any other way?"

Elanor shook her head.

I closed my eyes for a moment and took a deep breath. "Okay. If we go to the cops with this, they will definitely lock us up until they figure everything out."

"Those girls only have a few hours. It may already be too late."

"Then we follow the lead we have." I grabbed the file. "Let's go."

Chapter 22

MORDECAI'S NEW PROPERTY wasn't far from town. The small cottage was deep in the woods. We parked just off the road, blocking the driveway, and crept closer. Our magic-enhanced vision making the best of the moonless night.

"Wait up," I whispered to Elanor. "There's a haze. A shimmer. Right over and around the house."

"Must be an inverted ward," she said.

We circled the house to the car port. A tarp covered most of a white sedan, its license plate removed. "Look familiar?" I said.

She nodded. "Yes. That was outside Mordecai's shop."

"And at the car crash, in the gravel lot," I said.

Elanor took my hand and her magic reached for mine. "May I?"

"Of course."

We linked. Warmth flowed from her touch throughout my body, but she was peering past the car at the house.

"This True Sight spell is amazing. I've got to nail this down so I don't have to keep borrowing it."

"I like it when you 'borrow' from me," I said.

Her lips quirked and she squeezed my hand. "That's a ward, but it's just for magic. We should be able to pass through without a problem."

I nodded. "Makes sense. They would have to block tracking spells from the family and the cops."

"We won't be able to tell if anyone's home until we cross its threshold," she said. "And we'll need to drop our spells until we're inside. Trying to force our way through with them running will create magical feedback and disorient us."

I nodded. We crept past the car to the side of the house. The screen door creaked when I opened it, and door handle turned in my hand. I looked at Elanor and let go of the magic. She nodded. I opened the door, and we stepped inside.

*****

Unsure of where the ward ended, we took a step forward, hand-in-hand. The living room was empty except for a threadbare couch and a blanket. The door slammed behind us. Something grabbed my shoulder and shoved me to the floor. Elanor had been thrown away from me. A ward crashed down around me. I was trapped.

"Well, well," said Victoria, stepping out from the kitchen. "I wondered if you had the guts to get involved."

"Where are they, Victoria?" I said, standing. "What have you done with them?"

She shrugged. "They're on their way to their destiny."

"You know that one of them is going to die," said Elanor. "Is that a destiny you want for them?"

Victoria smiled. "Who lives and who dies is not for me to say. It was my job to procure them, and I did so, flawlessly." She walked forward and sat down on the couch. "And if you want to me to feel bad about it, you're wasting your breath. I mean, ultimately this is all your fault. You know that, right?"

Elanor and I looked at each other. "We know this all seemed to start at the Ferguson house," she said.

"It started when you killed my sister, bitch."

My eyes bulged. "Sarah? You're the missing twin?"

"Got it in one," she replied. "But I don't go by that name anymore. Not since I got my new lease on life."

"Your sister, Emily, was already dead when we found her," said Elanor.

"She was ghosted," said Victoria. "But she was still there, linked to me. I could feel her. Sometimes I even talked with her." Her hands clenched into fists in her lap. "You took her away from me. And what's worse is that you made it look like I lost her. I've spent my entire life in a backwater town, being the best Link I can be. Following all the rules. You took that all away from me in an instant. I thought they would discard me. And there were many, many things I planned to do to whoever took everything away from me."

Victoria stared at her hands. I took the moment to bring up my True Sight spell. Victoria's ward looked flawless, but weak. Of course. She's maintaining a ward on both of us and the ward on the house.

Victoria looked up. "But now I almost feel like I should thank you. I thought being a Link was my destiny, and disposable if it came down to it. But coming out here, into the world, meeting Mordecai. I have a lot more options than I thought." She smiled. "So to celebrate my good fortune, I'm going to kill one of you quickly."

Elanor crossed her arms. "So you have no problem with the fact that you've murdered two innocents?"

Victoria walked over to her. "Elanor. Sweetie. I can live my life in the great big world, with an unlimited credit card, pretty much forever. Literally."

I couldn't Send to Elanor, but I spun my finger through the air where Victoria couldn't see it. Keep her talking.

"Are you suggesting," Victoria continued. "That I should give all that up because of two local yokels with poor fashion sense?"

I can't test for a weak spot. I've only got one shot.

"And what about the poor kids that you kidnap? The families you rip apart? It happened to you and your—"

"Sister? Yes, it did. And I couldn't do a damn thing about it."

A knife might cut it, but she'd react, and it might not be enough.

"But he showed me a way. A way that still makes more sense than anything in this world. A way that my parents never could."

I gotta pop it like a balloon. Hit her with the feedback. I popped a small globe, keeping its light hidden in my hands, and began pouring an ocean of magic into it.

"Your murdered parents? Is that who you're talking about?"

"You shut your mouth."

"How could they possibly show you anything? Mordecai murdered them before they had a chance."

The light gleamed between my fingers like a flare. Sweat dripped from my forehead and my arms vibrated with the concentrated magic.

Victoria laughed. "Mordecai? You think he's behind all of this? You poor thing, I thought you were smart. He's killed people, sure, but he's nothing compared to the Savior."

"The Savior? Who's that?"

"Oh, it might be fun to introduce you. Briefly. But he doesn't want to talk to you. Your boyfriend however…." Victoria turned and stared at me. "Oh sh—!"

I let the globe go. In a blink it filled the ward enveloping me and shattered it. The globe expanded outward, ripping the wards around Elanor and the house to shreds. Victoria shrieked and stumbled. The force of the torrent took the strength from my legs and I dropped to my knees, the room spinning. Victoria raised a hand towards me, her face twisted in rage, magic flaring. Elanor stepped behind her, grabbed her by the shoulder. There was a loud pop-pop-popping sound and Victoria's body spasmed before she hit the floor and lay still.

"Thanks," I said as I teetered to my feet. "What did you do?"

Elanor rubbed her hand. "A low pulse of elemental lightning." She nudged Victoria's still twitching foot. "Well, maybe not that low."

"You tasered her?"

She smiled but said nothing.

"How long will she be out for?"

Elanor shrugged. "I don't know. Normally a minute or two, but on top of the feedback from blowing all those wards, could be a half-hour?"

I nodded. "Okay, I'll tie her up and we can lock her in the trunk of the car outside. You have a look around and see if there are any clues about where to go."

I tore the blanket from the couch into strips and began restraining Victoria. She flopped like a rag doll, but her breathing was steady. By the time I finished, Elanor came back, carrying an old leather-bound tome.

"Got something?" I asked.

"Yes," she said. "The entire thing is in an ancient Fae script. This must be the Pitokwe."

"Can you read it?"

"Not very well. Luckily there's a cheat sheet." She waved a piece of paper full of diagrams and scribbled notes.

"So, what's the next element?"

"Air," she said. "The notes say that they must complete the sacrifice while air surrounds the victim."

I frowned. "That could be anywhere, if Mordecai has the strength to use telekineses."

She frowned. "There are some notations here about acceleration. And needing at least fifteen seconds."

"That sounds like they plan on dropping her," I said. "Off a cliff. A big one."

"They must be heading to the mountains, but where?"

"Do you know Mordecai's aura enough to track him?"

"Yes, but remember his aura is connected to that tree in his office. The only tracking spell I know won't work with two identical targets, it's not sophisticated enough. The girls will be warded so…."

"What about the tracking stone with the golem's aura?" I asked. "Or the Savior's aura, or whatever it is."

Elanor's mouth twisted. "It's the most foul thing I've ever touched, but maybe I can get a lead on it."

*****

Together we dumped Victoria, still unconscious, in the trunk of the white sedan parked outside the house. As we returned to Elanor's car, she handed me the keys.

"You drive," she said. "I need to Send to my father. The authorities have to be told what we know." She sighed. "And I'll need to concentrate to do the tracking."

I nodded. "Good thinking. Someone might spot Mordecai's car on the road."

We got in and I started the engine. Elanor opened the leather-bound tome on her lap and popped a small globe. The car bounced on a rock as I turned it around.

Elanor frowned at me. "You got your license, right?"

"Yes, dear," I said, grinning.

Chapter 23

THE CAR'S HEADLIGHTS PIERCED the night as the tires ate up the road. The touch-stone's aura still sickened me, even though I wasn't touching it. Elanor held onto it for as long as she could before the aura faded. The golem was on the move, heading towards the mountains.

Elanor leaned back in her seat and sent to her father. It was nearly a half-hour before she opened her eyes again, shaking her head.

"You got through okay?" I asked.

"Yes. He was... weirdly accepting of almost everything I told him."

"Weird? How so?"

"He's always argues with me about everything," she said. "Once I had his attention and started laying out the facts, he just... listened. And he believed me, without question."

"Is he able to help?"

"Yes," she said "He's alerting the state police, claiming that we're government informants. He said that terrorists often target public places with cultural connections, in case that helps."

"Cultural connections? Like a place a tourist would hit?"

"Yes. Why?"

"I think I know where they're going."

I pressed hard down on the gas, and we hurtled towards the mountains.

*****

I pulled into the gravel lot of Blowing Rock State Park. Rivulets of magic trickled through the entire area. Ahead, up the walking trail to the cliff-face, lightning flashed purple and green.

"Good thinking," said Elanor.

"Thanks." We got out, and I handed her back the keys. She caught my hand and held it.

"I'm scared," she said. "But I'm glad to be here, with you. I don't want to be anywhere else."

In that instant, I could tell she spoke a simple, honest truth. My chest trembled as my heart raced. I embraced her. "I love you."

She stared at me for a moment, beautiful brown eyes wide with surprise. Her face lit up and she kissed me, hard.

Our magic connected. Blossomed. Fused. A calm descended on me, like nothing I had ever felt before. For an eternal moment there was nothing but her and I. We broke the kiss, but the connection endured.

"After this," I said.

"Yes."

We turned and faced the walking path, and hand-in-hand ascended.

*****

The smell of ozone gusted past as we broke through the tree-line onto the exposed granite cliff-edge. Elanor warded us, tapping into our shared magic with ease. I popped the True-Sight spell, but there was so much magic flowing the world was a blur of colors and I dropped it.

The kidnapped twins stood, arms outstretched, by the cliff's edge. A haze of oily black smoke whirled around them, unaffected by the wind that blasted past. A crackle of lightning snapped out from the golem to the ground, and a pulse of magic flowed under our feet.

"Magnificent, isn't he?" Mordecai shouted. He walked forward and stood between us and the twins. "Such power. Such control."

"You can stop this Mordecai," I shouted. "Call off the golem, it's over."

Mordecai laughed. "Golem? You think that he is a mere golem? That's the Saviour, boy! Your saviour, if you'd let him." He held out his hand to me. "There's still time. Come join me, the both of you. Drop your defenses. I promise he will spare you. Elanor, there's so much more to learn, and Cassius, he can bring out your full potential. You can be who you were always meant to be!"

We held our ground. "Not this way," I said. "Not with innocent blood on our hands."

"So be it," said Mordecai. A bolt of lightning leaped from his hand and shattered on Elanor's ward. The sharp crack of the discharge deafened me. Spots danced before my eyes.

Elanor's voice floated to me through our link. Cast the eye enhancer, it will protect you from the glare.

Mordecai was laughing "A ward. Not unexpected for amateurs, though well built. I should applaud your efforts but it will not avail you."

I cast the spell and a globe. My vision cleared. "Well, if you like our defense, how about our offense?" I pulled up a wave of magic, filled the globe to burst and hurled it at him. He waved his hand, and the globe veered away, smashing onto the ground and discharging a flash of light.

"Pathetic. Also not unexpected, given your lack of training."

The hairs on the nape of my neck stood up. A lightning bolt blasted against our ward, which rippled in protest. Magic poured through me as Elanor re-wove our shield.

"By the way," Mordecai said. "Do you know why I could tell you about twin-casting?"

"Because your ego wouldn't let you shut up?"

He smiled. The magic flowing to Elanor stuttered. She choked, hands grabbing at her neck. The ward faltered, unraveled.

Help me Cas!

I popped the True-Sight spell. A tendril of force pierced the ward where the lightning bolt had cracked it and wrapped around Elanor's neck. The veins in her forehead bulged and her eyes rolled back.

A tsunami roared in my ears. The keening of the wind died and slowed. Mordecai reached for me with another lightning bolt, his face frozen in triumph. I formed a shield, and watched as Mordecai's bolt slammed into it, coruscating into the air.

I formed a sword and slashed through the tendril choking Elanor. It recoiled, spluttering magic. I grabbed the end, and like shoving my arm up a sleeve reached through the tendril and grabbed Mordecai by the heart.

The wind howled. Mordecai's face flipped from triumph to surprise to fear. "How?" he sputtered. He fell to his knees, clutching his chest.

"Cas!" Elanor grabbed my arm and I pulled her up. "I don't know how you did that, but you can't."

"He was going to kill us!"

"His death won't stop this!" She pointed at the golem. The Savior. "That thing feeds off death. If you kill him, it will have enough energy to complete the spell."

Mordecai's laugh was cracked with pain. "She's right! And if you don't, he'll complete it anyway. You've lost!"

The whirlwind of oily smoke around the kidnapped twins slowed. Two balefire eyes opened. It stared at me. Through me.

What will you do, Weaver?

The voice oozed through my head, fouling my every sense. I wretched. The Saviour laughed. One twin floated into the air.

This is the one that I will bind to this place. Then your mate will die. Then you. Are. Mine.

Darkness descended, the world faded away. There was nothing but....

Elanor.

Her warm, golden glow guided me. I gasped, and the world swam back in to focus. We knelt on the granite rock, wind whipping past us, her large, fear-filled eyes focused on mine.

"Snap out of it Cas! We've got to do something!"

I had nothing. Nothing but our... connection. The Savior. He was still a golem or a ghost. He had to be connected to a living host. There. An artery, inverted and hidden, pulsing with life and magic. It linked Mordecai to the Savior, and throbbed in sync with his every heartbeat.

I formed a sword and slashed into the artery. Mordecai's screams reverberated through my chest. The Savior's darkness tried to drown me in an oil slick. I screamed, and the tsunami poured through me, washing away the darkness, the pain, the despair. The artery resisted for a moment before the tidal wave crashed down and clove it in two.

Mordecai collapsed. The Savior screamed in pain and fear, its smoke form dissipating. It whirled itself into a ball and tore off into the sky. The ground shook with magic as the binding spell unraveled. Elanor ran towards the twins, catching the one before it fell, huddling with them against the storm. The unravelling magic spun and whined. A final lightning stroke leapt to the heavens and split the night as the energy discharged.

The night air my lungs labored to fill themselves with was moist and cool. Elanor smiled at me. In the distance, police sirens wailed. The twins were safe. Elanor was safe. I was alive.

I stumbled over to Elanor and the crying girls, and hugged them all.

"Enjoy your victory," said Mordecai. He stood next to the cliff edge, staring into the distance after the Savior. "Enjoy each other, while you can."

I reached for the magic, but I was dry. Elanor wove together a ward, but Mordecai shook his head.

"I've done many terrible things these last three hundred years. But that's nothing compared to what's coming." He pointed at us. "Now, because of this, you will all die."

He spread his arms, stepped back over the cliff-edge and fell into the night.

I looked at Elanor, our hearts beating as one, our love driving out the darkness from our minds. "Whatever comes," I said. "I love you, always."

"And I love you."

We leaned forward to kiss. A searchlight split the night, pinning us to the rock face. The wind swirled and the chop-chop-chop of a helicopter buffeted our bodies. Armed men swooped down on rope lines, surrounding us. A soldier stepped forward and took off his helmet.

"Dad?" asked Elanor.

To Be Continued...

Afterword

Many thanks for your time spent reading Rights of Passage. It has been an amazing journey for me thus far, with two more books to come!

If you are able to spare a few minutes more, any feedback you can provide through a review on Amazon or Goodreads would be greatly appreciated.

Part of the creative process is cutting out those scenes which, though interesting, may slow the pacing down. There were several scenes in this book which I removed because the Point-of-View character, Cassius, was not present.

I expanded one of those scenes into a short: "Mordecai" is yours, free! Here's the link:

https://dl.bookfunnel.com/b963ts2ptf

Warmest regards
Doug Parker